Junglerama

Other Apple paperbacks
you will enjoy:

Goodbye, My Wishing Star
by Vicki Grove

Family Picture
by Dean Hughes

The Broccoli Tapes
by Jan Slepian

The Elephant in the Dark
by Carol Carrick

Bummer Summer
by Ann M. Martin

Junglerama

Vicki Grove

AN
APPLE
PAPERBACK

SCHOLASTIC INC.
New York Toronto London Auckland Sydney

ISBN 0-590-43163-3

Copyright © 1989 by Vicki Grove. All rights reserved. Published by Scholastic Inc.,
730 Broadway, New York, NY 10003, by arrangement with The Putnam Publishing
Group. APPLE PAPERBACKS is a registered trademark of Scholastic Inc.

12 11 10 9 8 7 6 5 4 3 2 1   1 2 3 4 5 6/9

Printed in the U.S.A.   40

First Scholastic printing, January 1991

*To Mike and his buddies,
as their spring
turns to summer*

Junglerama

•One•

The last night of May there was a ring around the moon, and the air was still and black as tar. The frog peepers in the ponds sounded like desperate drowning humans. Thinking back, I probably could have figured out from that first strange night that we were in for a weird summer.

I hadn't been wild in the first place about sleeping in Easy's tent that night, but he and Mike wanted us to make plans for the Whingding the next day.

"Hey, Teej, you're not scared again, are you?" Mike asked when I hesitated.

His hands were on his hips and his elbows flapped impatiently back and forth, back and forth. Sweat plastered his dark hair to his forehead and the red bird on his ball shirt to his chest. If you didn't notice the letters underneath, ST. LOUIS CARDINALS, you might have thought he had a massive chest wound. He was smacking his gum, looking hard at me with squinted-up eyes.

Easy Jack crouched between us, elbows on his knees, just whistling softly and looking at the ground.

Well, I saw this movie once where these three guys were camping in the woods, and in the middle of the night a hairy monster—I think it was Big Foot—squashed their tent to pieces and tore them to shreds. But try explaining something like that to Mike. He's just likely to laugh at you.

"Can't a guy even have a second to think quietly around here?" I muttered, my neck burning.

Mike shut up then, but he still looked at me with that smile he uses when he wants me to know I'm being a big chicken.

So I didn't say another word. I just went quietly along with the tent plan, all the while crossing my fingers that Big Foot wouldn't leave the Great Frozen North to venture as far south as Missouri.

• • •

It was hot that night in the tent and, like I said, the sky was black except for that strange ringed moon. We lay on top of our sleeping bags, trying not to jab each other with our elbows.

"Tilt-a-whirl," said Easy, opening the Whingding planning discussion.

"Definitely," Mike agreed.

"Right," I said, making it unanimous. We all knew that was the easy part, the only choice that would be clearcut. The tilt-a-whirl has been our favorite ride since about first grade, when we passed the point of getting sick from it. Choosing the other rides and games would be harder. After all, the Cloverton

Whingding only comes one day a year, the first day of June. And our money was hard-earned and tight. This called for lots of careful thought.

"How about the basketball toss?" Mike's voice was fast and sure and excited. He just loves getting things organized. I didn't offer an opinion, waiting, as usual, for Easy.

"Nah," he said. "We can shoot baskets any time at the school."

Of course, you didn't win prizes at the school. But since Easy was the only one of us good enough to win a prize anyway, if he said no, no it was.

"Tilt-a-whirl again," suggested Mike.

"Hmmm. I don't know. What do you think, T.J.?" Easy asked.

I stared out the open tent flap, at the triangle it made of Missouri night sky. Our feet stuck up like dark tombstones against it.

"How about the Haunted Palace?" I whispered, listening to the gagging frogs in Myers Pond down the road.

"All right!" Mike agreed immediately. Then, "But you won't chicken out, will you, Teej?"

Easy raised himself up on one elbow, and I could feel he was looking in my direction.

"Hey, Mike, give me a break. I won't chicken out," I said. I was glad it was too dark for them to see me. I could feel my neck turning red, again. Sometimes I've wondered if there's a pill or even an operation or something to cure your neck from doing that.

"Sure you won't, man," said Easy softly.

"So that's the tilt-a-whirl twice, then the Haunted Palace. We'll probably just have money for hot dogs and Sno Cones and one more thing," Mike figured, jiggling his feet impatiently. "How about the tilt-a-whirl again?"

"Sure," said Easy, after a couple of minutes.

"Yeah, okay," I agreed.

•   •   •

I woke up when it was still dark and they were both asleep. I'm always waking up in the night like that, because of strange noises and stuff. I snuck over and looked up once more at that weird moon, then closed the tent flap. I weighted it down with one of my shoes so that Big Foot couldn't smell us as well if he was out there, sneaking around.

Then I just lay there thinking about the summer ahead. Maybe this would be the summer that I would finally do something outstanding. Like, maybe I'd make the Babe Ruth team this time. Mike had pitched for it for two years. Or maybe I'd go off the high dive at the pool. Easy had a box of diving medals.

I was thinking around like that, almost asleep again, when something hit the side of the tent with tremendous force. I grabbed onto Mike, figuring we were about to be shredded.

"Go on, Teej," Mike muttered, still mostly asleep. He shoved me away, and covered his head with his sleeping bag. "It's just a stupid turkey lost in the dark. Don't be such a wimp all the time."

"I'm not," I said halfheartedly, but it was kind of

hard to talk because my heart was still jumping around like a bullfrog in my chest.

If I could have talked better, I might have tried to explain to him that it wasn't just the turkey. It was the stillness and the strangeness of that whole night. Even now, clear in August, when I try to remind them of the moon and the frogs and the strangeness of that first official night of summer, Easy and Mike don't remember it being that way. They think I'm just adding junk from my imagination to a normal night.

But it's the honest truth—stuff felt that night like the beginning of a horror movie, when you don't know what's going to happen but you know it'll be really gross and scary for the guys involved when it does.

• • •

The next morning we stuck around Easy's place to help him with his morning chores and then headed downtown, where the Whingding was already going strong. When we were a couple of blocks away, we could see red and white banners roping off a big chunk of Main Street, from the grain elevator clear past Ray's Clean Used Cars. Games and rides were packed in a wild hodge-podge along the street and sidewalks inside those flapping banners, and the smell of cigars and caramel corn got stronger every step we took.

"There! Tilt-a-whirl!" Easy said suddenly, throwing up one arm to point toward where bright turtle-shell chairs spun on a gray wooden track. We could hear the exciting carnival sound of people screaming their heads off inside those chairs.

We could hardly wait to get there, and ran the rest of the way. But when we ducked under the banners we were in for a big surprise. Because right off the bat we saw there was a new game this year. A goldfish game.

I've thought a lot about that game since. What was it doing there, anyway? I mean, I'd been to twelve Cloverton Whingdings altogether (counting the first one when my mother took me in my stroller) and there had never—I repeat, never—been a goldfish game before. Considering the weird stuff that happened later, considering the strangeness of the moon the night before, considering how much the fish we won had to do with things changing . . . well, all I can say is it makes you wonder.

"One thin dime, boys," called out Junior Tubbs, who usually pumps gas at Hinman's Texaco, but like all the other men who work downtown runs a game or ride on Whingding day. Inside his rickety stand was a cardtable packed solid with tiny fishbowls. "One thin dime in any bowl will win you a fish."

"Hey, you guys, those are real fish!" Mike said, yanking down on the brim of his Cards hat so it shoved his black hair into his eyes.

Easy just laughed, shook his head, and gave Junior a friendly but definitely not interested wave.

But Mike didn't budge to follow him, which kind of shocked me. We always follow Easy. Instead, he fished in the lining of his hat, then stuck a crumpled, smelly dollar out toward Junior. I knew from the awful looks of it that it was one of the dollars he hoards in his emergency savings account, in the toe of his old tennis shoes far in the back of his closet.

"Okay, give me change," he said eagerly, bouncing on his heels.

Junior had on this big apron thing to hold change in, but it wouldn't really stretch over his belly, so he had it tied underneath. His belly hung over it like something gooey and sliding, but caught in his T-shirt. He reached deep into the apron, then poured a fistful of dimes like glittering gravel into Mike's cupped hands.

"You lucky," I told Mike. Easy and I watched him take practice swings—under and up, under and up. Then his first dime sailed quick and easy into a bowl holding a black-spotted fish.

"Yes!" Mike said, punching the air and pivoting once around.

"Great," Easy said, and I could see real appreciation in his deep eyes. "Now, ask Junior if he'll keep it while we ride."

"You lucky," I repeated, a little louder. Mike was the only one with extra money that day, but he doesn't take a hint all that well. I finally had to spell things out. "Hey, Mike, loan me one, okay?"

He turned and narrowed his eyes at me for a second. Then he sighed and made his left hand into a dime-dispensing machine and dispensed one onto the countertop in front of me.

"One, remember," he said. "And don't waste your

shot, Teej. Put some power in your arm. And keep your eye steady."

I threw my dime, but the wind caught it so it missed.

Mike threw another dime and it balanced for a second on the rim of a bowl, then tilted in. He made it look so simple.

"All right!" he said, thumping the counter happily with his fists.

"Uh-oh," Easy said quietly then, and Mike and I both looked at him quickly and followed his eyes to the sidewalk a few steps behind us.

Matt Heims and the Tyler twins were standing there, hands in their pockets, T-shirt sleeves rolled as if they had muscles to show off. They were watching us like we were little kids, though they're only one puny year older than us. As usual they looked ready to pester any available human beings into being miserable.

"Hello, infants," said Matt, and Daryl and Carl laughed. You could see a package of Red Man chewing tobacco through the flimsy pocket in Carl's shirt. "Trying to win a little fishy-wishy? Isn't that sweet."

"Come on, you guys," Easy said quietly. "Leave us alone."

Matt and Carl and Daryl stepped off the curb and walked slowly to stand right behind Mike, crowding him so he couldn't have aimed right if his life depended on it. Carl and Daryl folded their arms across their chests and stuck their hands in their smelly armpits, and just stood there edging closer and closer to Mike, being obnoxious. Matt stepped to Mike's side to grin and leer at Junior, a few inches across the counter.

"All right there, boys, who's got a dime to win a fish?" Junior asked nervously, wiping the sweat from his pudgy face with the back of his arm. "One thin dime, right into the bowl of your choice, and you take home the whole kaboodle, fish and bowl and all."

"Hey, Junior. Why don't you go on a fish food diet?" Matt whispered into Junior's face, then leaned over the counter and spit at the ground between Junior's boots as his two buddies cracked up, bent double laughing.

"Funny, Matthew. Funny, funny," Junior said. But he walked to the other side of the stand, and stood by himself, his back to us and his head kind of sunk into his neck like a turtle pulling into his shell.

Mike and I automatically looked at Easy then, relying on him to get us out of this.

"Hand me a dime, Mike," Easy said then, quietly and steadily. Mike immediately handed him one.

"The one just left of the middle and back four rows, with the split tail and black-ringed eyes," Easy said, just loudly enough to get everyone's attention.

Junior perked up and hurried back toward us.

"Jack, this ain't no pool hall here," he said quickly. "You don't have to call your shots to win. Shoot, nobody'd take home one of these little fellers if you had to do that. Just get her in any old bowl, that's all."

But Easy didn't act like he even heard. He held

the dime in front of his face for a second, then flipped it through the air. It slid through the sky and arced edge first into the bowl he'd aimed for without so much as making a splash in the water. The split-tailed fish looked in surprise at the dime sinking slowly to the bottom of his bowl, in about the same way Matt and Carl and Daryl were looking at Easy Jack.

Mike took another dime, and I could tell he was trying hard not to smile when he turned around and held it out to Matt.

"You want to call one?" he asked Matt, innocently.

Matt swallowed once, then spit. This time, he missed the ground and hit his shoe.

"Hey, we got better things to do than hang around here watching the infants play, right, boys?"

And then the three of them slunk off through the crowd, their shoulders hunched and their elbows out, jabbing people who got too close.

"I bet you couldn't do that twice," Mike said, grinning at Easy.

Easy let out his breath and leaned with his knuckles on the board in front of him.

"Man, I'm glad I don't have to," he said, laughing a little.

"I could have won one if the wind hadn't caught my dime," I told them.

I immediately wished I could take that back, because they gave me that look that goes right through to my skeleton. Easy's eyes were clear and friendly, as always, but Mike's smile was fakey and he was shaking his head. I felt my neck burning, and I knew my hair was sticking to my forehead in sweaty spikes that looked exactly like carrots.

"Well, I could have, maybe," I said again.

Easy threw an arm around my shoulders.

"Time to quit with these fish and ride the tilt-a-whirl," he said.

We rode the tilt-a-whirl, like we'd planned, then decided to go to the Haunted Palace, then to ride once more.

"This is probably so fakey it's pathetic," I told Mike and Easy as we stood in the line outside the Palace.

It didn't take a genius to figure that out. You could see it was really just a big trailer truck, with pictures of vampire bats and screaming girls and wolfmen howling at orangish moons painted all over the outside. Scratchy horror music and screams blasted from speakers by the ticket stand.

"Fakey," I repeated.

• Two •

Still, to be on the safe side, I slid between Mike and Easy Jack as we ducked through the strips of rubber that hung down over the entrance.

We groped our way through a bunch of twisting dark aisles, and once in a while a strobe light would flash on and you'd see a horror mask with the eyes lit up. Sometimes the floors heaved and groaned, and we tried to be scared. But I'd basically guessed right—none of it was very scary.

Until we stumbled out the exit ramp, into the twilight.

And there standing in the shadows, leaning on her creepy, old colored walking stick, was the Toytaker. Her scrawny neck was bent so much that her head loomed forward like it was on a spring, long coils of gray hair flying from it in all directions. A skinny cat was wrapping itself in figure eights around her ankles.

"So you like to be afraid, heh, boys?" she cackled.

The Toytaker, in the daylight! I'd known that ringed moon meant we were in for something!

Before I knew what they were doing, my legs were pumping away a mile a minute, taking me back across town like a bullet. I didn't even have time to wonder if I looked to Mike like I was being stupid. All that pounded through my skull was getting away from that old witch.

I ran flat out like that till I got clear back near Junior's stand, and then I bent double with my hands on my knees and tried to get my breath back. Junior was groping in our three goldfish bowls, almost getting his fat hand stuck as he fished for the dimes on the bottom. He looked surprised to see me.

"Where's your friends?" he asked guiltily.

I ignored the question.

"Hey, that's cheating!" I wheezed at him between pants. "We're supposed to get the winning dimes back, too!"

"Take the darn things then, dimes and all," he grumbled, taking out his wet hand and shaking it through the air. "See what I care. You try to be a good game manager, and all you get is guff."

He hunched up his shoulders, and slunk off, over to where Peggy Simms was jumping up and down at the other side of the stand, waving a dollar bill in the air.

About that time Mike and Easy came up behind me.

"Hey, why'd you take off like that, Teej?" Mike asked.

I knew he'd just have to ask that, even though he knew as well as I did.

"You know why I ran, Mike," I muttered, staring

at Peggy Simms. She was hurling dimes wildly and recklessly. Junior had taken cover in the far corner of the stand.

"Well, we've still got forty cents each. No, fifty cents, counting the dimes in the bowls," Easy said then. "Anybody want to ride the tilt-a-whirl again?"

"I'm not going back to where that old witch is," I blurted out, then swallowed hard.

"Oh, come on, Teej, you're always imagining stuff." Mike grinned and gave me a friendly punch on the arm. I could tell he knew I was almost mad, and was trying to be jokey. "Mrs. Beeson's no witch. She's just an old lady. Tell him, Ease."

But Easy just planted his elbows on the counter and bent over to closely observe his fish. He stuck one finger in the water, and the fish came up and nosed it.

"Hey, Ease? Come on, tell him!" Mike prodded, kicking Easy's shoe.

Easy still didn't say a word. He was thinking, though. You can count on that with Ease. He's always thinking.

"Toytaker. The old Toytaker," I said in a whisper.

I thought I saw Easy Jack's jaw muscles clench. And yeah—Mike looked scared for a second, too, in spite of his brave talk.

Everybody, Mike included if he'd just admit it, knew Mrs. Beeson was a Toytaker, and everybody was basically scared of her. She moved to town when we were in second grade. She moved into the creepy shack that Mr. Harlan died in, which everybody knew was surely haunted, since they didn't find his body for five days. It had been empty (except for his ghost, of course) out there on Thornberry Lane since we were practically babies. Raccoons had lived in style there for years. The place didn't even have electricity. Then Mrs. Beeson moved in and started burning an oil lamp in the front window each night.

The house was creepy enough dark, but even creepier with that jumpy, gloomy light leaking out of it like it was a UFO or something. She planted a huge, wild garden all around the house, and flowers and weeds grew together very tall and dense, and animals and stuff lived inside the tangle. Creepy, noisy forest stuff. There didn't seem to be any way into the house anymore, or any way out.

But she must have gotten out somehow, because we started seeing her at night. She roamed the alleys, her colored walking stick going TAP, TAP, TAP, a gob of cats following her. At least, they looked like cats. They might have been monsters, though, just disguised as cats till they needed to assume their true shapes. Some kid at school had heard that kind of thing was possible and told the rest of us about it.

And some other kid figured out she was a Toytaker, a witch who snuck around in search of the toys of children. Or in search of the children themselves. Or maybe she got the toys and used them to lure the children. He, the kid (I think it might have been Tim Harmon, I don't remember for sure), wasn't positive how that worked. But his Toytaker name stuck.

"Toytaker, Toytaker—Zombie, Ghost, and Ghoulmaker," the kids on the playground at school started chanting to their jump rope and ball games.

After about a year of that, the novelty wore off. But you heard a grown-up blame her once in a while when a cow didn't give milk, or when somebody lost a pair of roller skates or something. And mothers would still call little kids in if she was walking around a neighborhood where they were out playing after dark.

Yeah, she'd been in town over four years now, but even some of the grown-ups were still afraid. So Mike wasn't so smart. He didn't know everything, even if he had pitched for the league last summer. Even if I did owe him money at the moment.

"I got an idea," Easy said slowly. "Why don't we just stay here and play for some more fish?"

"Yeah," I agreed immediately.

"Okay, sure. Why not," Mike said, pulling his change from his pocket. "I guess I'm not exactly raring to go back there myself."

• • •

So we played for about another half hour, until finally our dimes were all lying in the sawdust under the fish table. By that time we owned a grand total of nine goldfish.

We were then faced with two big problems—how to move them and what to do with them.

We sat on the curb to think.

"Mom probably won't want fish," I said, picturing her turning bright pink and yelling at me if I even asked about them.

"Mine either, probably," said Mike.

We both looked at Easy, the only one without a mother.

"Well, we shouldn't try to keep them in my tent," said Easy. "Lots of cats prowling in the neighborhood."

That gruesome thought silenced us for a few seconds.

I glanced over at Junior, who was glowering at us, his elbow on his stand by our nine lined-up goldfish bowls. You could tell he was impatient for us to move the fish, which were taking up counter space from the paying customers.

Suddenly, Mike jumped to his feet.

"There, you guys!" he said, pointing excitedly down the street. "There's my sister's car! We can put them in back and Molly can give them a ride home!"

Well, it looked to me like Mike had solved the moving part of the problem, but the mother part was still left hanging.

"But Mike? Your mom," I called to him. He'd already reached Junior's stand and was loading his arms full of splashing bowls.

"You guys can come home with me and help talk her into it, okay?" he called back.

Everybody knows mothers have a lot harder time saying no in front of people that don't belong to them, so we agreed.

•Three•

We snuck napkins from the hot dog stand and packed
the fish bowls carefully so they wouldn't clank together and possibly wouldn't get Molly's floor wet.
Then we hit out walking for Mike's house.

It was hard leaving the Whingding just as the colored carnival lights were showing up so well in the
growing darkness. The lights and the loud music
made the town appear more alive than it ever does in
real life. Usually, Main Street seems more tuckered
out than anything the last couple years, like the
sleeping dogs that dot it on August afternoons. So
many stores have closed down and are sitting empty.

I just live a couple blocks off Main Street, so when
you're walking to Mike's from downtown you go right
past my house. My stomach started hurting the second we turned the corner and started down my block
that night. My mom had been in a terrible mood for
a few weeks, and I wondered if we'd be able to hear
her yelling. Usually you could hear her several
houses away. And if it was dark, like now, there was a

good chance you could see her, too, standing in front of some window waving her arms and throwing clothes around. She did ironing for people then, and always had plenty of clothes handy to throw.

Usually, she was angry at one of my sisters, or at me. But that night, when we got a little close, you could clearly see my dad smoking his pipe and sitting in a chair in an upstairs room, while she paced behind him, slapping chairs with a shirt as she went. My dad's back was to her and he faced the street, but his shoulders were hunched like a dog hunches before a switch.

I wanted to say something to drown her out, but I couldn't think of anything, and we heard some of what she was yelling.

". . . expect us to live on air now, George? On air, on nothing? Just tell me what the plan is, okay? Why should I be the one to always worry and stew and lose my mind when we get in a mess like this?"

Easy started whistling real loud then, and Mike beat time along with him with his hands on his jeans. I tried to whistle, too, but my mouth felt too dry.

Finally, after what seemed like about six years, we were past my house and around a new corner. Easy quit whistling and glanced over at me, and I shrugged my shoulders, like it didn't matter. He smiled and shrugged back.

· · ·

When we got close to Mike's trailer, we could see there was a pickup truck parked outside.

"Dad! Dad's back from Wichita!" Mike yelled, and

ran ahead of us the last half block or so. He took the wrought-iron steps in one leap, and yanked at the door so it flew open and practically knocked him off his feet. Then he remembered us.

"Come on, you guys! Hurry!" he yelled.

You couldn't blame him for being excited. Mike and his family used to live on a farm, but his dad sold their house and land last winter, and now he worked all over the place—Little Rock, Tulsa, you name it. This time he'd been gone working in Wichita for a whole month.

We ran too then, and crowded into the trailer right at Mike's heels.

"Hey, Bud! Howdy there, boys!"

Mike's dad looks just like a big version of Mike— straight black hair, blue eyes that crinkle at the corners, even freckles which is something you don't see every day on a grown-up. He was sitting at one of the chairs at their kitchen table, his long legs stuck out and crossed at the ankles. You could see part of a horse's head tooled on each of his boots, where they stuck out from under the edges of his jeans. His wide-brimmed hat was on the table in front of him, and there was a jagged band of dried sweat above the snakeskin band around it.

He pushed back his chair.

"Come here, pardner." He laughed and Mike ran and grabbed onto him, half wrestling, half hugging. Mike quickly got him in a stranglehold and pulled him sideways, so they overturned the chair and fell to the floor, still laughing and grunting.

"Oh, so you want to play mean, hey, Bud? Say, I'll show you mean. Yes sirree, I'm right about to show you mean."

Easy Jack and I flattened ourselves against the door. There wasn't much room in that trailer, especially with Mike and his dad thrashing around on the floor like that. Still, it was hard not to egg them on.

"Tickle him!" I yelled. "He hates that!"

Mike's dad grabbed Mike's foot and yanked off his tennis shoe, and began tickling him to beat the band. Mike was laughing so hard no sound was coming out of his mouth, and he just kept helplessly kicking the air with his free foot.

"Please!" he wheezed once, then just kept laughing and croaking breathlessly.

"You give then, Bud? Let's hear it. You give?"

"Give!" Mike yelled, tears running down his face.

"Oh, man!" Easy Jack shook his head, disappointed.

Mike's dad let go of his foot and Mike got to his knees, then grabbed for the table and got his father's hat, holding it far out behind him.

"I'll spray it with Molly's hair junk! And her worst perfume, too!" he yelled, trying to quit laughing enough to make it to his feet. "I will! You give?"

"Way to go, Mike!" Easy laughed and clapped his hands, his eyes bright.

"Boys, now . . ."

All four of us looked up in surprise. It was the first time since we'd come through the door that we noticed Mike's mother was in the room, working quietly over the sink.

"Small space in here," Mike's dad said, looking sort of sheepish. "We'd best settle this down."

He got to his feet, slowly brushed off his shirt, and went to put an arm around Mike's mother's shoulders.

"Hey, Dad? How long are you staying this time?" Mike asked excitedly.

Mike's mom turned quickly back to the sink, and his father's arm dropped heavily from her shoulders.

"Well, son, that's hard to say," he said, rubbing his forehead with one big red hand. "Maybe a week, maybe less. There's this guy with a ranch out near Tulsa that's needing some help for a few weeks, and that could start any time."

Mike didn't say anything, just gulped, his eyes frozen on the snakeskin band of that hat. We were all quiet for a minute. I wished there was something Easy or I could do, like Easy and Mike had done when they made that noise when we passed my house so we wouldn't hear my mom yelling. Mike was proud his dad was a cowboy—who wouldn't be? But Easy and I also knew how much he missed his old farm, and his family being together on it. He'd been hoping his dad would be home this summer, since he'd been gone at that ranch in Wichita for so long.

We all just sat there and listened to the water going through the broccoli in Mike's mother's strainer for a couple of minutes. Then Mike's dad came over and put one hand on Easy's shoulder, and one on mine.

"Hey, boys, I hear the Whingding was today! Did you all have a good time? Say, I want to hear some happy talk around this place. What's been goin' on in this old town while I've been gone?"

Mike jumped to his feet, his eyes flashing. "Dad, there was this game there, this goldfish game? I don't think they ever had it before. And Junior Tubbs, he was running it, said to this other guy—and we heard him, didn't we, guys?—that nobody had won more times than we . . ."

I was getting a little worried, wondering if Mike had forgotten his mother was in the room and we hadn't softened her up yet. But it turned out not to matter.

Because suddenly the conversation was drowned by the noise of an old engine clattering to a loud stop just outside the door. And then there was the sound of stomping feet and the thick metal door of the trailer banged open.

Molly was standing there, her hands on her hips, glowering at the three of us as though she could vaporize us with her eyes.

"All right, all I want to know is who is responsible for turning my perfectly dry and clean car into a damp and smelly . . . a damp and smelly . . . aquarium!" she fumed.

We just stared at her, trying to decide whether we should stand our ground or make a run for it. Then, lucky for us, Molly realized her father was home, a fact she'd been too mad to realize when she almost ran right into his pickup parked outside.

"Daddy!" she cried, running to his arms and stretching up on tiptoe to bury her face in his neck. "Daddy, Daddy, Daddy!"

"Come on!" Mike hissed at us, and we slunk down and followed him from the middle of the action. We were just about to make it to the narrow hallway leading to his room, when his mother turned quietly and caught him with her eyes.

"Mike?" she said softly. "Fish?"

He ducked his head and looked down at where his right tennis shoe was pushing up the linoleum a little with its toe. "I'll take care of them, and the guys will help me, Mom. I promise."

Easy and I nodded solemnly.

"Them, Mike? How many?"

Mike looked at Easy, and Easy looked at me. I looked at Mike, and we all three shrugged.

"I don't know. How many would you guys say?"

"Just a . . . few," Easy answered.

"Hardly any," I agreed immediately.

"Maybe . . . maybe nine," Mike said.

His mother took a deep breath and let it out as she went back to swishing around those vegetables.

"We can give it a try, I guess," she said after a couple of long minutes. "But, Michael, this is a small place. You boys must promise to keep them clean, or the whole trailer will smell fishy. Do you promise that?"

"Thanks, Mom!" Mike yelled, and he ran across

the kitchen, out the door, and jumped the porch. Easy and I were right behind him.

• • •

It took us about another hour to organize the fish in Mike's room. It was amazing how much space nine bowls took up. You could hardly walk in there.

"They would have had gobs of space in my room in my old house," Mike said once.

Then we remembered they needed food. They were hanging around the tops of their bowls, sucking air, looking.

Mike's mother gave us some bread. They looked at it suspiciously at first, but finally ate it. Tomorrow Mike said he would get some real food at Jensen's Variety, after his dad gave him his allowance.

Molly's car was hardly damp at all, in spite of her carrying on. We took a towel out and sponged a little, and everything was good as new. Still, his mother made us apologize to Molly and promise we wouldn't put things in her car again without asking.

Fat lot of good that would do. All of us knew she would never in a million years have let us if we'd asked.

•Four•

When we left Mike's, it was almost nine o'clock. I knew I should go home, but every time I thought of that I could see my mother in front of that lighted window, slapping that shirt at my dad and yelling. And besides, I'd have to travel alone through several dark, creepy blocks to even get there. Sort of like swimming through a shark pool to reach the electric chair.

"You going home, Easy?" I asked when we got to the edge of Mike's yard.

"Yeah," he said. "Guess I better get things checked for the night."

I nodded. Then I just stood there.

"You going home, Teej?" Easy asked.

"I guess," I said. I knew my voice sounded wimpy. I was glad Mike wasn't out there with us to hear.

Then I just stood there some more.

"Okay then, so long. See you tomorrow probably," Easy said, and started walking off into the shadows toward his edge of town.

"Yeah, see you." But I just stood there. I couldn't make my feet go.

I was wishing I was like Easy, cool and strong. I was wishing I could pitch like he and Mike pitch, and I was wishing I could go on home and wrestle on the floor with my dad and have my mom laugh kind of quiet and nice about it. Sort of be pretend mad, instead of real, shirt-slapping mad.

"Teej? Hey, want to come along to the tent and see my Ozzie Smith card?"

Easy was standing about half a block away, his hands in the pockets of his jeans, one foot stuck out a little in front.

"Will Judd care?" I asked.

Easy laughed. "Hey, you know Judd is probably asleep in one of the bars downtown by now."

"Sure, then. Yeah!" I said, and ran to catch up with Easy.

• • •

Easy's parents died when he was real little, and ever since he'd lived at the edge of town on his uncle's rare bird farm. Judson's Bird Emporium, it was called. Judd, Easy's uncle, was one of the custodians at the Cloverton Elementary School, and he ran the Emporium on the side. His dream, he kept telling us, was to start a mail-order company for the rare and not-so-rare birds and turkeys and chickens he raised. He had lived on this neat island called Haiti when he was a kid and had known somebody with that kind of business. But he didn't seem to know exactly how to go about starting one up, so he put it off and just let the birds keep laying eggs and the flocks keep getting bigger and bigger. He had a couple of acres filled with bird cages and pens of all shapes and sizes, all of them covered with knocked-together wooden flat-topped buildings to keep the weather out. But by last spring he'd completely used up his space. The chain-link fence around the Emporium looked like a skinny man's belt worn by a fat man. Something had to give.

That something turned out to be Judd and Easy. Judd gave the biggest room of their house over to a new crop of baby turkeys. After a week or so Easy took to sleeping in his pup tent in the yard because the turkeys made too much racket in the night and started perching on his feet.

Easy and I walked toward the Emporium without talking for a couple of blocks. Beyond the block of trailers where Mike lives, there get to be fewer and fewer houses, until finally they peter out altogether. We were almost out of houses and at the place where the Emporium was sort of carved out of the woods when Easy finally spoke.

"I couldn't believe it when I opened that pack of baseball cards and saw old Ozzie there, holding that bat and grinning. I didn't think you'd ever get that good a card in the packs the grocery store sells."

"You were lucky," I told him. "Had the bubble gum soaked through?"

"No. It was perfect. Not even bent."

Boy, it sure was dark out here at night, I noticed then. Last night when Mike and I were out here there was that weird ringed moon, but tonight there didn't seem to be a moon at all, which, if Easy hadn't been with me would have been too spooky to tolerate. I hadn't noticed how the birds sort of moaned in their sleep before, either.

"Hey, Ease? Are you ever, you know, scared or anything?"

He stopped walking, partly because we'd reached the big gate on the chain-link fence, and partly to think. Easy has this habit of thinking quietly before he talks a lot of the time.

He stood there with his hands on his hips, a good five inches taller than me, muscles already in his arms. But I knew his face would be friendly, if I could have seen it in the dark.

"Hey, T.J. Sure I'm scared sometimes. What do you think?"

Then he opened the gate and swung it wide enough so we could both get in, and closed it behind us. There weren't any lights on in the house. Judd always turned a bunch on before he went to sleep, so I figured Easy must have been right about him being gone to some bar or something.

"Nope. No Judd tonight. Come morning, I'll walk to town and bring him on home," Easy said.

Then he led the way through the dense darkness to the place where his tent was set up between the quail pens and an incubator building. He dropped to his knees and crawled through the flap, and I followed. He started rummaging in the stuff he keeps in one corner for his flashlight. When he found it, he turned it on and rummaged some more for his shoe-box full of baseball cards.

"Like, when are you scared, Easy? 'Cause, see, it doesn't seem to me like anything could ever scare you." This next thing was real hard for me to say, but suddenly it seemed important to get it out in the open. "I mean like today, I ran when I saw the Toytaker. You and Mike didn't, but I just couldn't stop myself."

"Yeah," Easy agreed. "You ran. That's okay. Here's my John Tudor rookie card. Want to see it again?"

"Sure." I reached and took it from him.

"Hey, T.J.," he said softly, his eyes on his cards. "Did you ever wonder how it feels to be black?"

To be black? I thought about that.

"No," I said.

"Well, in a town like this, with only six other black people altogether, sometimes it feels scary."

I sat, taking that in.

"You mean it's scarier than being flesh-colored?" I asked, not sure what he was talking about.

He turned the flashlight on me and looked straight in my eyes. I shrugged to tell him I really didn't know what he was getting at.

"Stop and think about it, Teej," he said quietly. "To me, I'm the one who's flesh-colored."

I stared at John Tudor as Easy turned the flashlight back on his cards and went on looking for Ozzie.

"You don't understand though, Ease," I said after a minute. "See, everybody looks up to you because you're good at sports and get all A's and everything.

So if you're like that, I figure it's easier not to be scared. But you can't get like that just by wishing you were, you know? And it seems like stuff is always happening, at home and stuff. Stuff that makes me wonder if I'll ever get it together and be like . . . you."

"Here he is! Get a load of this, T.J. My man, Ozzie."

He handed me the card and the flashlight.

"Wow."

We sat quietly appreciating it for a few minutes, with the birds snoring and moaning around us. I was sort of hoping Easy hadn't been listening to the last stuff I'd said. It sounded little-kid jerky to me now when I remembered it. Kind of whiney or something.

"Hey, Teej?" Easy said suddenly, his voice sort of low and hoarse. "Okay, I tell you what. When we get the cards put away and the flashlight off, I'll tell you something that really scares me."

My heart started beating fast. This was going to be good.

• • •

"My Uncle Judd, you know, was born on the West Indian island of Haiti. In fact, my dad was born there, too. They were boys there, lived in a house made of reeds and palm leaves and stuff, on the edge of a loud, bright jungle."

We were lying down now, stretched out, our arms folded under our heads, staring at the chicken coops and the stars through the open tent flap.

"And Judd talks to me sometimes about that island, about the steamy heat and the green palms, the blue water and the bright red dresses his mama wore. I can tell Haiti must have been a place where people laughed a lot. Judd says they even caught fish with their hands, the water was that clear."

"Wow." I stared at the plain old navy blue Missouri night, thinking of all that moving jungle color, all that water and sand. It would have been neat to think about it longer, to ask Easy to describe it more. But other things were more pressing just then.

"But Easy, you said you were going to tell me something scary."

He just stayed still for a few more seconds, and I thought I heard him swallow hard. Then he pulled slowly up onto one elbow and bent toward me.

"There was something else there, in that jungle, Teej," he said, whispering now. "Something terrible and mysterious. I haven't told anybody this. Not even Mike."

I could feel prickles on the back of my neck. I pulled my feet up under my knees, out of the opening of the tent.

"Drums, calling through the jungle night," Easy went on, his voice so quick now and quiet that I could tell he'd thought about this a lot. "The moon so orange you wanted to jump up and eat it. And women in white dresses, dancing, chanting, their shell jewelry hissing through the darkness and their arms weaving the night over their heads. The dancing, the drums, calling villagers to the jungle, to the fire, to . . ."

Easy stopped. His mouth was open, and I could see by the starlight sneaking into the tent that his eyes were wide, focused not on me any longer but on something inside his head.

"For Pete's sake, go on, Ease!" I practically yelled, sitting up.

He kind of shook his head and focused his eyes back on me.

"Voodoo, Teej," he said in a fairly normal voice. "Voodoo."

"Voodoo?"

"Voodoo. Jungle spirits called loas, priests and priestesses called mambos, leading people in worship to the loas around jungle fires. Animal sacrifices in the night, people going into trances and walking into fire, and horrible hexes put on someone by the giving of a gift."

"Whoa." I slid farther back into the tent, grabbed Easy's rolled-up sleeping bag and wrapped it around me. I'd never heard Easy so wound up, except maybe about diving the summer he won his medals. And even that he didn't go on and on about like he was this.

"How do you know that stuff?" I whispered. "Did Judd tell you?"

Easy shook his head.

"Nah. Judd won't talk about anything after he talks about the dancing and the fire and says the word 'voodoo.' It always freaks him out, partly 'cause he's usually pretty drunk before he brings up the subject of Haiti in the first place. I looked the rest of that stuff up in the library. It was in a book I found, *Primitive Religions.*"

Easy stretched back out, and I huddled under his sleeping bag and wondered how he could stand to sleep out here alone every night, with all this voodoo stuff in his head. In fact, how was I going to make it five blocks to home tonight?

"That's not the scariest part, Teej. The scary part is the zombies. The walking dead. Their mouths are sewn shut so they won't tell about the horrors of the underworld. The mambos raise them from their graves, and they can ruin a whole village with powerful magic."

My throat felt like an inner tube was stuck in it, but I finally managed a whisper.

"You don't believe that stuff really, do you, Ease?"

"I'm pretty sure Judd does," he answered.

"Yeah, but you don't. Do you?"

Easy sat up and crawled over by me.

"You know, T.J., sometimes it's like this jungle drumming just starts in my head when something scary happens. Like when we saw the Toytaker today, I mean. I don't exactly believe in voodoo, but still, how could it all be just made up when my uncle and my father were right there, doing it and seeing it? I don't know. It's hard to explain."

Easy did a good job of covering, but that voodoo stuff scared him. He'd pretty much admitted that. I didn't like the idea of anything being scary enough to scare Easy.

"I better go," I said, knowing that if I didn't get up and run right then I might not be able to. "See you tomorrow."

● ● ●

I was halfway home, running too hard to have to figure out how scared I was, when I saw her out the corner of my eye, luckily a good block or so away.

The Toytaker, walking in the darkness through our town. Followed by a swarm of cat monsters, and probably the ghost of Jeremiah Harlan.

The Toytaker, roaming like a quiet zombie through the night.

I turned my legs into pistons and put on a burst of speed that I hoped against hope would jettison me out of her field of vision before she zapped me into mincemeat.

•Five•

I was probably going about a hundred miles an hour
by the time I turned the corner on my block and
charged toward the house. All the upstairs windows
were lit up, though it must have been ten o'clock by
then. I took the six porch stairs in two strides, threw
my weight against the front door, then nearly broke
my neck over something small and solid someone had
left in the hall.

It turned out to be my sister, Cassie. She was
crouching there in the gloom, sucking her thumb,
her eyebrows two worried lines above her green
eyes. When I came to a screeching halt half an inch
from her, she stood and silently raised two sticky
arms for me to pick her up.

I started to ask her where Mom and Dad were, but
then I heard their angry voices from up in their room
pouring down the stairs like torpedoes or something.
So I just put my finger to my lips, picked up Cass
and tiptoed upstairs with her, to where I figured
Mame would be waiting in their room.

Usually, I get both of them ready for bed, especially on tense nights like that one. That night I knew they both needed baths. Mame was so sticky I had to peel her clothes off her like you'd peel a banana. And Cassie smelled kind of like the refrigerator smelled that time Mom didn't pay the light bill and all our food spoiled. But I didn't want to waste time with that, and I didn't want to make the noise it would have made. The torpedo barrage from down the hall was exploding in my head, and I knew the quicker the rest of us were undercover in our beds, the better.

"I want my mama," Cassie whispered firmly when I'd tucked her in and stuck her teddy bear under her arm. "And I want her *now*."

"Hey, give me a break, okay?" I said. I could see her round eyes were swimmy, but I wasn't feeling all that cheerful myself at the moment. And it would have taken the energy and courage of a superhero to go in and get Mom right then.

"Okay, I'll give you one," Cassie said with a huge yawn, then rolled on her side and shut her eyes.

"All right!" I whispered, thinking that sometimes Cassie could be a really neat little kid, for a three-year-old.

Mame is still only a baby, really, and she had been asleep on the floor of their room. She didn't wake up when I undressed and changed her and put her in her crib, which was cool.

When I finally got to my own room, I thought about reading comics or counting my arrowheads or something. After such a confusing day, it would have been nice to give my brain something to unwind with. But the noise from down the hall just kind of bored into me, and made everything seem too hard. So I stripped to my underwear and got in bed.

I watched the elm tree in front of the streetlight making the light move around on the ceiling for a while, but the noise from my parents' room didn't stop like it usually eventually does. Finally, I got up and went to my closet to get the set of broken earphones I thought I might still have in there. Sure enough, I saw the tangled cord hanging out from under a pile of junk. I crouched and started yanking them out. But before I could get them, and get them on my ears so I didn't have to hear anything much anymore, I heard my mother's voice clearly through the flimsy closet wall.

"Not your fault, not your fault. That's all you can ever say. So what now, George? I tell you, I've had it! I'm fed up! How am I supposed to raise these kids with you without a job now? Without a job in this miserable town without jobs?"

I got the earphones on quick after that, and ran and dived into bed again. I crossed my arms over my head to give my ears an extra layer of stuff to not hear through.

I knew what they'd been arguing about from hearing those few sentences. There had been talk around town for months that the meat-packing factory where Dad worked might close, and I guessed it had finally happened. My dad had lost his job.

My mind kept trying to think about my parents down the hall, but I knew there was nothing I could do to get that factory to open back up. So I forced it to think instead of other things. I wouldn't let it think of the Toytaker either, or that voodoo stuff of Easy's. I needed to settle my brain on something I could get to sleep on.

The fish.

I started thinking about the fish we'd won. Or Mike and Easy had won, actually. Then I thought that maybe I'd start saving my lawn-mowing money and go to one of those pitching camps they have down in Florida or in California, one of those places. Anyway, maybe I'd go for a week or a month and come back a star pitcher.

Only who would get my sisters to bed? Well, maybe I could take them with me. It wouldn't be the ideal situation, of course, but it would probably work out.

I was getting dozy, almost out of it, when I remembered Sparky and jolted awake.

Sparky is probably the best person in my life, even if he is a dog. Even counting Easy and Mike. And though I'd trusted my mother to feed him while I was at Easy's and then the Whingding that day, I had a feeling with all this stuff about my dad's job she might have forgotten.

I ran to the closet and dug out one of the jerky treats I keep hidden there for Spark. Then I tiptoed downstairs and out onto the back porch. He was standing there, wagging his stub of a tail, like he expected me.

Still, he didn't exactly bounce all over me that night like he usually does. He stood there with his head tilted, staring at my head and frowning, looking seriously worried.

It was then I realized I still had on those headphones, the long cord hanging down from my head like my brains were leaking out or something.

• Six •

When I woke up the next morning, the house was too quiet. Our house is never the least bit quiet. I lay in bed for a while, hoping for some noise.

And then something told me to look outside. I looked down at the yard, at the toys scattered around through the grass, the broken fence that was hanging there where one fencepost had worked out of the ground. I looked at the tire swing with the big dusty space underneath it. And then my eyes moved to our oil-splattered driveway, and I felt like an empty glass with sadness pouring into me, cold and clammy.

The driveway was empty. My dad had left in the night.

I knew I should go check on Mame and Cassie, but I just had to get out of there.

I jumped into my jeans and T-shirt from the day before and ran, down the stairs and out the door, toward town. Sparky was right at my heels.

• • •

When Sparky and I got to Main Street, we saw
there was a whole lot of clanking and banging going
on. Men were taking down the rides and games from
the Whingding, packing things up into trucks and
trailers. Litter was blowing through the air like feathers at Easy's place, and it caught against the fenders
of the cars.

I'd come to town, hoping to see my dad's truck
parked by the post office or the bank. When I saw it
wasn't anywhere around, I suddenly felt too awful to
move, and sat on a curb and just watched the sham-
bles around me. Sparky kept licking my neck, like he
always does when I'm feeling down.

We didn't even notice Mike till he sat down beside
us.

"Hi," he said. "Hey, Teej, you look awful, like that
flour and water paste we made in art last year. No
offense."

"Thanks a lot," I told him. But that's exactly what I
felt like. Flour and water paste. I laid back on the
sidewalk and sighed, my arms folded under my head.
"No offense taken," I muttered.

Sparky went over and nosed Mike to say hello, and
Mike grabbed him around the neck and hugged him.

"I came downtown to get some fish food," Mike
said.

I looked up at the sky for a few seconds.

"I came to get away from my stupid house," I said.

I was afraid he'd think that sounded wimpy and say
something, but Mike only frowned thoughtfully and

nodded. He had a tennis ball with him, and he started throwing it against a nearby stop sign.

A couple of minutes later a screen door slammed right down the block, and a burst of laughter and off-key singing made all three of us look in that direction. I sat up, forgetting for a second how miserable I was. It looked like Easy's Uncle Judd and a couple of his buddies were coming out of the Tip Top Bar, swaying as they tried to find their ways home after a night of sleeping at their tables.

Sparky took off like a shot toward them, and it was then Mike and I saw Easy behind Judd, sort of guiding him by the elbows.

"Hey, Spark!" Easy said, stooping to give him a good rub. Sparky immediately rolled over to stick up his stomach, and Easy took the hint and rubbed that too. The three old men stood there watching, chuckling.

"A good loyal dog is truly one of the finer things of life," one of them said, then belched and stumbled a little.

Easy sat down on the curb beside us, pulling his uncle along with him by the shirtsleeve. Judd seemed happy to sit and rest, and smiled at us as he took out his handkerchief and mopped his face. The other two old men lifted their hands to wave more or less in our direction, then they drifted on down the sidewalk, singing their tuneless song.

"T.J. is having a rough time," Mike said to Easy.

Easy looked at me.

I shrugged. "I guess."

"And you guys," Mike continued, "I gotta tell you right out that having our fish at my house, my trailer I mean, is getting to be an uphill battle. Molly came into my room this morning, with those roller things in her hair and smelly cream on her face, and she threatened me."

Wow, a threat! That was interesting enough that it broke clear through the funk I was in, and I leaned toward Mike.

"What?" I asked eagerly. "What threat?"

"Well, she said if she smells even the slightest fishy smell in her room, she's gonna put fingernail polish remover in their water."

"Wow!" I jumped to my feet. "Hey, Mike, you can't let her do that! That's got to be against the law or something, isn't it? I mean, that would kill them, wouldn't it? Wouldn't it, Ease?"

"Most likely," Easy said, in that quiet, drawn-out way he has of talking when he's mostly thinking. "What we need, ideally, is a place where we can all get to them to protect them and watch them and stuff. I'll do some thinking, and you guys do, too. But right now I got to get my uncle home to his bed."

Easy Jack got to his feet, and pulled Judd up, too. But Judd shook Easy's hand away and stepped into the street, in front of all three of us.

He swayed a little, standing unsupported there. He looked sweaty and smelled awful, and his cheeks were all yellowish and sunken in. But suddenly, his eyes were full of excitement.

"You boys say you're needing a place to start you

up some fish?" he asked, his voice husky. "Say, I got you just the place. Oh, yes indeed I do!"

Then Judd began walking quickly down the street. Some of the blowing trash from the Whingding caught on the legs of his pants, but he didn't seem to notice. The cool morning wind seemed to have cleared his head a little, that and his mysterious excitement. He clamped his old gray felt hat onto his head with one hand.

"Well, you boys coming?" he asked, stopping half a block away to yell back at us.

We looked at each other. "Well, come on, you guys," said Easy.

• • •

We followed Judd for about three blocks, to the end of what had yesterday been the midway of the Whingding. The Haunted Palace, the tilt-a-whirl and Ferris wheel, the line of ring toss and balloon and dart games were all gone. Only overflowing green trash sacks marked where they'd been.

Besides trash, the only thing left on this block of the street was a little junky trailer. It had a couple of flat tires, and most of the glass in its windows had been broken and taped back together. A bunch of bees buzzed around a big dribble of something that looked like a melted grape Sno Cone drying on its open door. Rust was eating spider-web shapes through the ugly grayish-green paint on the trailer's sides.

A big piece of dirty brown cardboard, about the size of a refrigerator box, had been taped clear across one side of the trailer. Someone had lettered the cardboard in bright orange—ART'S CARNIVAL NOVEL-TIES. On the other side of the trailer was a grubby display counter.

All in all, the place looked like it was just sitting there hoping somebody would haul it off and push it over a cliff.

Judd went over to the trailer, kicked the two totally flat tires a couple of times each, and then looked up at us, grinning.

"Well, boys, believe it or not—she's all yours!" he said.

Easy frowned at Judd and folded his arms across his chest, like he does when he's trying to figure something out.

Mike was just standing there in shock, his blue eyes totally round, his mouth a little open.

I myself was trying to remember back to yesterday. I remembered seeing a skinny, jittery-looking man sitting in this trailer during the Whingding. He glared at Easy and Mike and me when we walked past on our way to the tilt-a-whirl, and I got the feeling he was about to reach out and snatch us and force us to buy some of the cheap souvenir junk he was trying to sell.

"Uh, Judd?" I said. "I thought this trailer belonged to one of those guys that was traveling with the carnival."

Judd rubbed his hands together and chuckled. He took a few prancing steps from the trailer and looked at it with pride as he talked.

"Well, it used to it did, son. It used to it did," he

said. "And that self-same man you mentioned came trotting into the Tip Top Bar while I was a customer there last night, looking frustrated as a crawdad in a bottle. And this here is what he says. He says, 'My name is Art Jugerman, and I'm sick to death of this carny life. I'll take me fifty dollars for that ugly green trailer down the street from anybody crazy enough to give it to me.'"

Judd stopped, shaking his head and grinning, re-membering.

After a couple of minutes, Easy said, "Uncle Judd? What happened then?"

Judd looked in surprise at Easy.

"Well, boy, everybody laughed at him, of course! But me, well, I thought he said fifteen dollars and that sounded like a fair deal. So I says, 'Stranger, here's your money.' And I stands and puts a ten and a five on the table in front of me."

Easy and Mike and Sparky and I could hardly breathe from wondering so bad what happened next. But Judd stopped his story as suddenly as he'd started. He went and sat on one of the fenders of the trailer, leaned back against the rusty metal, pulled his hat down over his eyes, and immediately went to sleep that way, still grinning.

"What do you make of all this?" Mike asked.

"I think Uncle Judd must have bought this trailer from that Art Jugerman guy for somewhere between fifteen and fifty dollars," Easy said, frowning thoughtfully. "And I think he just gave it to us to keep our fish in."

Mike and I jerked our heads over to Easy. At his words I guess the true wonderful potential of the trailer just sort of sailed into our brains, knocking everything else out.

"Wow," I said, pretty much stunned. "This could be where we spend our time this summer. I'd hardly ever even have to go back to my stupid house."

"Yeah," Mike breathed. "We could even sisterproof it with booby traps and stuff!"

At that moment, Sparky suddenly stood up perfectly straight and still, trying to use his stubby tail to point like a real bird dog would have. He was looking with extreme suspicion at something directly behind our backs, and the three of us turned around slowly.

Matt Heims and Carl and Daryl Tyler were working their way toward us, down the cluttered street. They'd been amusing themselves, it looked like, by prowling around through the trash-filled bags, kicking them open with their boots. Carl bent down and picked up something in the garbage he must have thought was a quarter, but it turned out to be a pop-top tab. He said something gross and spit.

"People are sayin' this piece of junk belongs to your crazy old uncle, Easy," Matt said as they got close to us.

"He's not crazy, Matt," said Easy. "Don't call him that."

Matt walked over to the trailer, took out his pocket knife, and started carving initials into the wood of the counter.

"Well, you can tell the law that Judd's not crazy,"

sneered Matt, "because I happen to know Sheriff Perlman's having the police give hundred-dollar tickets to anybody leaving a mess out on this street. The sheriff's giving everybody till noon to get junk moved out, or else."

He ran his knife under his chin at the words "or else," then closed it with a snarly laugh.

"Come on, fellas," he said to Carl and Daryl, who had fished a broken plastic key ring out of the trash and were looking it over carefully. "We warned these infants, now we got more important business elsewhere."

They took off back down the street in the direction they'd come, kicking sacks as they went.

"Yeah, you guys better steer clear of Sheriff Perlman yourselves, or he might see the trash mess on your boots and the trash mess on the street and put two and two together," I muttered.

"Oh, cool, Teej. Way to go. Wait till they're too far away to hear, then really let them have it!" Mike laughed.

Well, of course, I'd waited till they were too far away to hear! You don't want to mess with them. They're just plain mean. I started to explain that to Mike, but he was leaning toward Easy, jiggling one leg impatiently.

"Now what do we do?" he asked. "I hate to say it, but I bet Matt's right about those hundred-dollar tickets, don't you?"

"Yeah," said Easy. "I think they do that every year. We've got to get this trailer moved, pronto."

"Well, it's not going anywhere with two busted tires," I observed. "Otherwise I guess we could push it to the Emporium."

"Can't keep it there," Easy said, his eyes squinted like he was moving his brain into overdrive. "It probably wouldn't fit through the gate. Anyhow, there's not a speck of room, and chickens eat fish, remember?"

We nodded solemnly, remembering.

"Hey, Mike, how about Waco's pasture?" Easy asked softly. "Any chance we could use a corner of it for the trailer?"

Suddenly, Mike didn't look so good. His freckles stood out against his skin like they had a life of their own, and his eyes looked like he'd been socked in the stomach.

He looked so bad that Sparky went and laid down on his feet.

•Seven•

Easy and I both knew Mike was real touchy about his old life, before his dad sold their farm. And Waco and his pasture were a big part of that old life.

When Mike's dad still farmed, they lived a couple of miles out of town on about 200 acres. Their house was real old, built by Mike's great-grandfather, I think. Or maybe his great-*great*, even. Mike loved that house. It was white, two-story, with a whole bunch of big trees in the yard and a big barn in back.

They had a lot of cows and the usual pigs and chickens. And they had one horse—a champion quarter horse. Waco. Mike's dad rode Waco in rodeos in the summers around here. Mike was learning to ride him, too, but then he got sold.

Mike's dad sold the house, the land, the animals, and Waco. But he kept the little pasture—just a couple of acres—where Waco had been corraled. It was down the road from Mike's old house, about a mile out of town.

Mike said he was sure his dad kept Waco's pasture because he meant to buy Waco back, any time now.

"My dad's a cowboy, after all," he was always saying. "And everybody knows a cowboy needs a horse."

So if Mike went and asked his dad about using that pasture for our trailer, and if his dad said it was okay, that would be kind of like saying Waco wasn't coming back, wouldn't it? At least not coming back right away.

I could see why Mike didn't want to face asking about it. I knew Easy could see that, too, and hated to make Mike feel bad. But we didn't have a whole lot of choice at the moment, unless we wanted that hundred-dollar ticket. We had to do something and do it fast.

Mike crouched down and rubbed Sparky, where he was still lying on his feet. When he straightened back up, he took a deep breath.

"Dad was gone this morning, but he ought to be back at the trailer by now," he said. Then he swallowed a couple of times. "I'll go ask him about it."

He didn't wait for us to answer. He just turned and took off at a run.

We watched him go till he was around the corner, then Easy turned to me. "Well, I guess the next thing's to get Judd home. I'll only be gone an hour or so. You stay here and guard the trailer till I get back, okay? By then maybe Mike will be back and we can figure what to do next."

We shook Judd by his shoulders so his head wobbled, and eventually his chin hitting his chest woke him up enough so that we could get him on his feet.

"What?" he said. "What?"

Easy put an arm around his waist. Judd put his arm limply across Easy's shoulders, and I watched the two of them shuffling clumsily back across town toward the Emporium.

Then I sat on the curb, and settled in to guard the trailer.

• • •

At first there was a bunch of noise, hammering and clanking from the guys still taking rides down. But then the workers must have quit for lunch, because all of a sudden the street looked deserted.

The bees buzzed around the Sno Cone mess on the door of the trailer and the ground underneath it. A bunch of flies gathered, too, where Matt's gang had scattered trash.

It was getting really hot, and I thought I could feel my brains cooking. It was just too quiet—that was the main trouble. And I'd seen a movie once about big bunches of bees attacking people and sucking out their insides. Maybe there were flies mixed in with the bees in that movie, too. It would have been hard to tell.

I watched my foot as it poked at tarballs in the gutter. I didn't want to look up and see the place right across the road where the Toytaker had been standing yesterday.

Suddenly, it sounded like the bees were right inside my head. I started wondering if some of them had snuck into my ears or something. Maybe they'd suck my cooked brains out. Or could they at least lay eggs in there? That would be even worse.

The wind came up, clammy with rain, and I shivered and jumped to my feet. I thought I felt cold hands around my neck. A few bloated raindrops hit the street and hissed, and a sheet of dark, greenish clouds ate the sun.

"Sparky?" I said, but he didn't hear. That was because no sound really came out of my dry throat.

"Hey, Spark?" I croaked again. He flicked one ear, but still slept.

And that's when I heard it.

TAP . . . TAP . . . TAP . . .

The Toytaker was coming up the side street! I should have known it—this was one of those storms that follow monsters, not a genuine summer storm at all! In a few seconds she would reach the corner and turn and see me, standing right out there in the open, guarding the stupid little trailer. The Toytaker and whatever ghosts and monsters she happened to have with her would catch Sparky and me out in broad daylight without another soul around to hear our final screams.

The tapping became so loud it woke Sparky. He was still lying on the street, but he had his head up, and was frowning toward the corner, growling slightly in the back of his throat. He sniffed the air, so I did too. It smelled putrid, like something rotting.

One good thing occurred to me. At least this would

make my parents sorry for yelling. Maybe they'd even hold hands at my funeral and would realize if they'd been nicer I wouldn't have had to get out of our stupid house this morning, and I wouldn't have been out here meeting my doom.

But what would I care how sorry they were? I'd be dead!

I looked around frantically for a place to hide. The elevator building behind me was locked up tight. The stores across the street looked locked up and dark, too, and besides there wasn't time to reach them. The Toytaker could zap me before I got halfway across the sticky asphalt street, and I for sure didn't want to end up breathing my last breath face down in a torn garbage sack.

I ran to the door of the trailer, and had almost decided to pick up Sparky and jump inside, but the bees stopped me. They were thick around the door now, blocking it.

And then Sparky had the answer.

I looked down at him, and he was half crawling, half slithering under the trailer. I hit the ground and rolled under there, too.

And then a shadow stretched itself onto the cracked sidewalk at the corner, and the tapping became unbelievably loud. It echoed in my head like an executioner's drum—BONG-BONG-BONG.

Then suddenly the tapping stopped. And so did the wind. Everything became eerily still. What light I could see from under the trailer looked greenish and weird.

The spooks must have reached the corner. If we looked up and saw them, I knew we were goners for sure.

Sparky looked at me, and I looked at him.

Then I covered his eyes with my hand and buried my face in his ear and tried to keep from screaming my head off.

•Eight•

I don't know how long we stayed that way, huddled under the trailer. Thunder crashed and the wind kept blowing, and once we heard something that sounded like the monsters were clawing away at the skin of the trailer right over our heads. Still, we clamped our eyes closed and didn't move a muscle. I kept thinking every second was our last.

Then I felt sweat dribbling down my neck and I realized it was hot again, so I opened one eye and saw the sun turning the puddles to steam outside. I heard noise too, hammering and laughing and stuff. The workers must be back from lunch! We weren't alone any longer, and somehow we had managed to survive!

"I think it's safe," I whispered to Sparky.

He hung out his tongue in relief, and started looking eagerly around. He saw Easy's feet before I did, and went slithering out to lick his tennis shoes.

"Hey, boy!" I heard Easy say.

I took a second to think about the situation, then

grabbed all the candy wrappers and Sno Cone cups I could reach.

I worked my way out from under the trailer, clutching that junk to my chest.

"Hi, Ease," I said, as calmly as I could. I got to my feet, dumped the stuff in a garbage sack, and started batting dirt off my shirt and jeans.

"Teej! What were you doing under there? I been looking all around for you!"

"I just was under there, you know, picking up trash and stuff," I told him. "Uh, is Mike back?"

"Not yet," Easy said.

I breathed a big fat sigh of relief, knowing Mike wouldn't have bought that trash story for one second. And I didn't exactly need to be laughed at right now. It had been a weird morning.

I was trying to decide whether to tell Easy about the flies and the rain and the tapping when I noticed he looked different. His eyes were sort of wide and flashing, and he had them glued to the side of the trailer.

"Did you see this yet, then?" he asked me in a rush. "Man, did you look at this?"

I turned around to face the trailer like he was, and I could hardly believe my eyes.

The whole side of the thing was pulsing with color, color that throbbed out at you and just about knocked you off your feet. Where before there'd been that big old piece of cardboard with Art's Carnival Novelties written on it, now there was a big picture painted right on the side of the trailer, about six feet long and maybe four feet high.

"The rain soaked off the cardboard sign," Easy said, his voice a hoarse whisper. He pointed down the street a little way, and I saw the soggy piece of cardboard where the wind must have sailed it. So that was the big sound of clawing I'd heard on the trailer! Maybe the spooks were ripping it off. Or, of course, I guessed Easy could have been right and it could have gotten wet and just fallen off.

"That sign has been covering this picture for hard telling how long," Easy said, still talking in that strange whisper. More like he was talking to himself than to me. "Lucky thing, too. Otherwise it would probably have had that same ugly paint slapped over it that's on the rest of the trailer."

I looked closer at the picture, then stepped back a few feet so I could see it better. At first it had looked just like bright, shiny, swirling colors. But from farther back you saw it was a jungle scene. Brilliant green and copper palm trees waved in a tropical wind with red, black, and yellow-striped snakes coiling through their branches. Tigers, rhinos, and giraffes peeked with wild eyes through dark shadows between the trees. And the head of what was either a dolphin or a very ugly mermaid rose smiling from the deep blue of a pool under the palms.

"Haiti," Easy whispered. "That must be how Haiti looks."

And then I saw there was writing on the picture,

big block letters. It was hard to see them at first, because they were sort of camouflaged in the leaves of the palms. One of the snakes' tails made the capital J.

"JUNGLERAMA," I read, running my hand over the hard, glossy letters. "Wow."

"The Junglerama," Easy repeated, still sounding like he was in a trance or something. "All right. Yes."

Right then, there was a clattering behind us, and Mike and his dad drove up in Mike's dad's pickup truck. I waved, but Easy didn't seem to be able to peel his eyes away from that picture. I'm not even sure he heard the pickup.

"Say now, this is really something!" said Mike's dad, leaning out his window and taking his hat off.

"Wow!" Mike said, jumping out of the truck and running to the side of the trailer.

"Great, huh?" Easy said, still not moving his eyes.

"I'll say," Mike agreed.

Mike's dad sauntered up behind us.

"You boys know what I'll bet?" he said. "I'll just betcha this trailer used to be used for one of those traveling animal shows. When I was a boy you'd see such things at the county fairs, and even sometimes at the little local street fairs like the Whingding. You'd pay a dime or so, and you could go inside and see wonderful rare fish and reptiles and such things. Usually they'd have a trained monkey or a baby bobcat or something like that they'd bring outside to entertain with, too. But it was the reptiles—lizards and snakes—that me and my friends paid our dimes to see. Too bad you don't see that kind of thing now. Seems like carnivals are mostly full of junk places these days, nothing to really catch your imagination."

"Ease?" Mike sounded worried, and I looked at Easy, too. He still had that dazed expression on his face. "Hey, Easy? Dad said we could use the pasture, and he's here to hitch the trailer up to help us pull it out there."

Easy nodded slightly, but it took him several seconds to speak. "Hey, call it the Junglerama, okay?" he whispered. "From now on it's not 'the trailer,' it's the Junglerama."

"Great. The Junglerama. Okay, Teej?" Mike asked, shifting his weight from foot to foot.

"Great," I agreed.

"Now come on," Mike said, shaking Easy's arm. "Let's get going on this before we get that ticket."

• • •

The three of us rode in the back of the pickup as we pulled the trailer out to Waco's pasture. Sparky rode in the cab with Mike's dad, sticking his face out the window and slobbering happily into the wind. Sparky loves pickups.

We traveled, going about two miles an hour because of the flat tires on the trailer, the rest of the length of Main Street, then turned off onto Thornberry Lane through the Toytaker's rundown shacky part of town. We finally reached the gravel road bordered by open fields just beyond the town limits. The pasture lay just beyond the sign that read CLOVERTON, POPULATION 2100. It was about a mile from the middle of town. From the Emporium, clear on the other edge of Cloverton, it was probably about a mile and a half. Easy would have the longest way to come to reach it, but still that wasn't far on a bike.

By the time we got there, after fifteen minutes of watching the trailer bump and weave behind us, we were all in a great mood and our heads were about ready to bust wide open with ideas. I had even almost forgotten how close a call I'd had under the trailer earlier, and even about my dad's pickup maybe being still gone. All I could think about was how neat the Junglerama was going to be. How perfect it would be to spend the summer out here with it, instead of in town where everything could get to you sometimes.

Mike's dad helped us get the trailer set up under a big cottonwood tree, then he drove off and left us there to begin making plans.

By the end of the afternoon, we had things about figured out. We were going to bring out a bunch of supplies and sleeping bags and stuff, in case we ever figured out a way to get our mothers to let us spend whole nights out here. And inside the trailer, we would build cages and find old bowls and things and start collecting a true jungle exhibit, like the one Mike's dad had told us about. Who knew? Maybe someday we'd even have enough good stuff to start a traveling exhibition of our own. We decided we might even take it to Arizona or Texas or someplace like that, and play the carnival circuit. We might even own an alligator. We might even get rich, or semi-rich, and become world-famous.

We wanted to keep making plans like that, but when it got dark we knew we needed to get home. Tomorrow we could start riding our bikes out when we didn't have lawns to mow, and we could run back and forth for supplies that way.

"We ought to make a pact," Easy said. "Right here at the start, we need a pact."

Mike and I nodded, and waited for him to go on.

He looked around. We followed his eyes, and looked around, too. The lights of Cloverton were coming on across the dark fields directly in front of us. Off to one side, over a small hill, you could see a glow in the sky that was where the new people now lived in Mike's farmhouse. To our other side was where the gravel road turned into Thornberry Lane.

So on three sides of us was civilization a few hundred yards away. But behind us was another story.

We all three turned around, probably thinking the same thing. We faced the dark woods behind us. We could hear birds and animals calling to each other back there. Talking to each other in languages so strange and foreign they made French and German seem just like baby talk. Lots of things were just waking up back there in the woods. Lots of life was starting its night rambling, slithering and creeping, open-eyed and watchful.

Easy raised his arms toward the woods, and closed his eyes. We did, too.

"We swear by our blood and our friendship. . . ," Easy began.

"We swear by our blood and our friendship. . . ," Mike and I repeated, trying to copy the flat, serious tone of Easy's voice.

"To be true to the spirit of the jungle . . ."

"To be true to the spirit of the jungle . . ."

Easy hesitated a few seconds, then went on.

"To keep its secrets and respect its ways . . ."

"To keep its secrets and respect its ways . . ."

Easy stopped again, frowning and thinking. I knew he was searching for a good end to the pact, but my arms felt like they were about to drop off.

"Or may we all fall down and rot in our tracks," I finally finished for him.

He and Mike looked at each other, then shrugged.

"Or may we all fall down and rot in our tracks," they said.

"Okay, you guys, that seals it," Easy said. "Now we're brothers of the jungle. When we're out here, it'll be like we're in a whole different world."

Mike and I nodded solemnly.

But now that the trailer was moved, and the pact was sealed, something like panic was washing across me. How many hours had it been since the first time I thought my mother was going to kill me for being gone so long? Six hours? Eight?

"I gotta go," I said, kicking at the gravel. "Immediately. I'll see you tomorrow, if I'm still alive."

"Wait up, Teej," said Mike. "I gotta get home too."

We looked back to wave at Easy when we got to the edge of the town. He was sitting in the grass, leaning against the side of the trailer, his head resting on the brightly painted jungle pool.

I wondered if he was hearing those jungle drums he had told me about. The ones that pounded in his head when he thought of Judd's stories of Haiti.

•Nine•

Mike was quiet walking home. I couldn't tell too well in the dark whether he was just being nothing-to-say quiet, or whether he was being sad quiet. Since I didn't want to think about what was waiting for me at home, I needed him to talk, like he usually did, and give my brain something else to settle on.

"Hey, are you okay and everything?" I finally asked.

He just kicked up some gravel and didn't answer.

"Hey, Mike? What?"

He shrugged and sighed.

"You know, T.J., I never did understand why we had to move in the first place," he said.

"From your old house to the trailer?"

"Yeah. My mom and dad don't talk about it. Molly doesn't talk about it, not that she probably knows any more than I do. It was just like, one day Dad and Mom called us into the kitchen and said some people wanted to buy the house and the land, and we were selling out while we had the chance. That's the phrase they used. Selling out 'while we had the chance.'"

"Well, maybe they got sick of driving into town when they needed something," I suggested. But I was pretty sure that wasn't right. I just couldn't think of anything else to say.

"Nah. I think my dad just wanted to try working as a traveling cowboy. But you know what Dad said today when I went to ask him about using Waco's field? He said, 'Sure, son. Glad to see that pasture used for something, now that Waco's out of the picture.' Out of the picture, Teej! I mean, I knew Dad sold him, but I figured he'd buy him back any time. And I guess I sort of thought maybe someday we'd go back to our other house, too, when Dad got sick of cowboying."

Mike stuck his hands deep into his pockets, and his shoulders slumped. He filled his cheeks with air and blew them out. "I don't get it. I just don't get it. The way they act it's like they don't plan on ever going back to like before," he mumbled.

We were at the beginning of my block. I tensed up and my stomach began to hurt. But the house looked dark. And nobody was yelling that I could hear.

For some reason, that scared me worse than Mom's yelling noise.

"See you in the morning, Teej," Mike said and cut across the street, his shoulders still slumped like that.

"See ya, Mike," I said. I wished I could think of

something to say to cheer him up a little, but I couldn't. I was too worried myself.

And Sparky wasn't much help. He'd been chasing rabbits all afternoon at the pasture and now he was dragging along at my heels, totally beat.

• • •

When I reached my yard, the quiet hit me like a ton of bricks, like it had when I first woke up that morning. I couldn't hear a single thing but the swish of the tire swing as I walked up the sidewalk to the porch.

Dad's pickup was still gone. I could see that much.

I opened the screen door and called: "Mom?"

But nobody answered. Nobody ran into the hall to tackle me around the knees, either. Where were Cassie and Mame?

My throat got tight. I saw this movie once where this man had razor blades for fingernails, and he snuck into houses at night and slit the throats of defenseless little kids.

I went up the stairs, trying not to make a sound in case somebody like that was lurking in the shadows. My hands felt numb, like they were on somebody else. I stuck my neck down in my shirt as far as I could. That was one thing—if I was going to get slashed, I didn't want them to get my neck, like in the movie.

Cassie and Mame were in their beds. I thought at first they were asleep, but when I tiptoed toward them, I saw all four of their eyes were round and wide open. They both were sucking their thumbs

real hard, and Cassie had her teddy bear smashed
upside down against her cheek, so his legs tangled in
her damp hair and his snout stuck into her neck.

"T.J., my tummy's hungry," she whispered. "And
Mame wet her pants."

I went over and lifted Mame from her bed. Sure
enough, it was soaked.

"Where's Mom?" I whispered as I scrambled
through Mame's drawer looking for clean pajamas. It
would have been easier in the light, but for some
reason I was afraid to turn the lights on.

"She's in her bed," Cassie said. "Daddy left, and
she's got a awful headache. She said she can't cope
and we got to shut up."

I finished changing Mame and stripping her bed,
trying not to act as scared as I was.

"Wait here. I'll be right back," I whispered to my
sisters, who sat side by side on Cassie's bed now,
looking like sad-eyed dolls. Mame sank over and put
her head in Cassie's lap, and Cassie smashed her
teddy bear into Mame's face, comfortingly.

I tiptoed down the hall. I was more scared pushing
open Mom's door, to tell the truth, than I had been
under the trailer earlier that day, waiting for my
doom to fall. That was pretty stupid when I thought
about it. Why would you be afraid of your own
mother? She wasn't even yelling.

"Mom?" I asked. "It's T.J. Are you sick?"

I could dimly see her on the bed, her face toward
the wall.

She didn't answer me.

"Mom?"

This time her shoulder heaved up and down, and she let out a sound sort of like a groan.

"I got the girls ready for bed, Mom," I said, swallowing hard. "Uh, Cassie says she's hungry."

And then I heard something awful. She was sobbing, low and kind of animal-like sobs. I'd hardly ever heard her cry before, not even the other times Dad had left. I kind of thought people who yelled didn't have to cry, or something like that. I knew some mothers cried. You saw that stuff on TV sometimes, moms crying about happy things or sad things. But those moms were a different kind of mother from mine, usually skinnier and just about always quieter. And when they cried they cried softly and daintily and used tissues. I didn't think there was a box of tissues anywhere in our house. You had to use toilet paper to blow your nose when you had a cold.

I suddenly realized I had to get out of there.

I would get out of there and run through the night, run to the Junglerama. That was it! I'd run to the Junglerama, to the world I was going to inhabit with Easy and Mike. And I'd forget all about my gone father and my moaning mother and my waiting sisters. They'd quickly fade from memory like nightmares faded once you got outside and started having fun.

I'd be free and happy, and I'd go to that baseball camp in California or Florida and then come back and help Easy and Mike get the Junglerama ready to take on the road.

That was just exactly what I'd do.

All I had to do was tiptoe back out the door of my mother's room, then I could make it down the stairs to freedom and never, never look back.

"Thomas James." My mother's voice stopped me, pinned me at the door. "Thomas, your father's left us again. This time more'n likely for good. Get your sisters some peanut butter and crackers, you hear?"

Her voice was weak and shaky. She wasn't even mad at me for being gone all day, and that really scared me to death.

"Yes, Mama," I said.

•Ten•

I took Cassie down to the kitchen and fed her those crackers and some milk, but Mame was already fast asleep when I went back to get her so I didn't wake her up. Cassie went right to sleep after she ate, too.

In my room I sat on the floor beside my window, thinking about all the lucky people in the world who weren't trapped in their stupid houses. I don't know how long I'd been sitting there, my chin on the windowsill, when Mike's dad's pickup came around the corner. He rolled to a stop, and Mike jumped out. I could see Easy sitting inside the truck, by Mike's dad.

"Hey, up here!" I whisper-yelled down to them.

"Come out!" Mike yelled back. "We got something we gotta do."

I shook my head.

"Come on, Teej, hustle!" Mike yelled again. "This is an emergency!"

I just shook my head again, and whisper-yelled

down, "I can't. I can't even come outside and talk. Things are awful here."

There's this big trellis thing up the side of our front porch. Roses used to crawl up it in the summer, but Mom didn't water them and Cassie dug sand cakes in the dirt around them and they finally petered out and died. Now that bare trellis is perfect for climbing up to the flat roof just outside my room.

Mike had finally gotten the picture that I couldn't talk loud, and he started climbing the trellis. I unhooked the window screen and pushed it out, stepping onto the roof to meet him.

"Teej, listen. When I got home tonight, Molly had put all the fish into a big, smelly pickle jar and left it on the front porch!" Mike said, breathing hard with anger. "And they were actually eating each others' fins! Being in that small space was turning them into cannibals, Teej!"

"Didn't your mom try to stop her?" I asked.

"She said I should have gotten that fish food so the fish wouldn't be starving like that," he muttered. "But she also said Molly had no right to take things into her own hands."

I looked down from the roof, and for the first time noticed that there was a big, round thing taking up practically all the room in the back of the pickup. And it had water in the bottom.

Mike followed my eyes, then turned back excitedly.

"It's Waco's old horse tank, Teej. My dad said we

could take it out and set it beside the trailer tonight, and put the fish in it. But it'll take all four of us to get it unloaded. Dad and I put a few inches of water in it with the hose, and now it weighs a ton. So come on, let's go!"

I looked back over my shoulder.

"Hey, really, Mike, I shouldn't leave," I said, but my feet were already moving toward the trellis. "Well, anyway, not for very long, okay?"

"Right," said Mike from where he was shimmying over the side of the porch.

• • •

Mike and I squeezed into the cab of the pickup beside Easy and Mike's dad. I was squashed against the door, so I looked out the window as we drove into the country. It was so quiet and dark I fished around in my brain for something to say to break the silence.

"It's neat out here at night," I said. "So many stars. Kind of peaceful or something."

"Right," said Mike's dad, with a sort of snorting laugh. He shook his head. "'Or something' about describes it."

I didn't get what he meant, but I could feel Mike tense up and jerk his head toward his dad in the darkness.

"It *is* neat out here, Dad," Mike said firmly. "It is peaceful, too. It's the best place in the world, the country is."

Mike's dad cleared his throat.

"I didn't say it wasn't great living in the country,

Mike," he said quietly after a couple of minutes. "But there's lots of problems with it, too. We were lucky to find a buyer for our place when we did, going more broke each season, working all day and worrying all night. I'd had about as much 'peace' as I could stand, and then some."

I was really wishing I hadn't brought the subject up. Easy rubbed his forehead and quickly said something about a new bunch of quails just hatched at the Emporium.

But Mike shoved his shoes flat against the floorboard of the truck, crammed his hands into his jeans pockets, and stared hatchet-faced out the windshield, not ready to let the subject drop.

"We could have hung on," he said, his voice so stringy I wouldn't have known it was him if he wasn't right there beside me. "Others have. You just wanted to try cowboying. You should just admit it, Dad."

Mike's dad jerked a little, like he'd taken an unexpected slug to the stomach. I could see the Jungle-rama then, half a mile or so ahead. Everybody was breath-holding quiet as we drove that distance. Mike's dad pulled the pickup off the road, under the cottonwood tree, and turned off the motor.

Still, nobody made a move to get out of the truck. I didn't want to turn my head toward Mike, but out the corner of my eye I saw something shiny about his eyes.

"Son?" Mike's dad said. "I don't know where you got that. I'm not a cowboy, not even a farmer now that I've had to give up my land. If I was a cowboy, I wouldn't have sold Waco, now would I? No, I'm just a guy trying to make a living for his family any way he can. When I go to Tulsa it'll be to help shovel out stalls for a big horse breeder there. Mike, I need you to accept me for what I am, not for what you want me to be."

Mike sat real still for a minute. Then he reached across my chest, yanked the latch of the door, and shoved it open. He scrambled over me, jumped to the ground, and took off running.

His dad jumped from his own side of the truck. "Mike, stop!" he yelled.

Mike was headed toward Thornberry Lane, though I don't imagine he had any destination in mind. I knew that feeling of needing to escape. Of going fast through the darkness without a plan of action, trying to outrun the things in your head.

"Let's go get him before he breaks his neck," Easy said, and he and I took off, too, running toward where we could see Mike disappearing down the gravel road, into the darkness.

• • •

Easy outran me, of course. He got to Mike first.

They were sitting when I reached them, their elbows on their knees and their heads down between their arms, panting. I dropped down, too, feeling like my chest was about to explode.

"Fake," Mike got out between breaths. "He's just a big fake."

"Did he ever actually tell you he was a cowboy, Mike?" Easy asked quietly.

Mike jumped to his feet, weaving like his legs were made of rubber. It took him a while to answer Easy's question.

"Well, he never said he wasn't one, either. And I thought . . . I thought . . ."

He turned so his back was to us and walked quickly into the shadows a few yards away. I looked at Easy to see if we should follow him, but Easy shook his head. We just sat there, staring at the ground.

"I think the meat-packing plant finally closed down this week," I said after a few minutes. "My dad lost his job. My mom ran him out."

I guess I thought it might help Mike if he knew other people were having father problems. Or maybe seeing him sad had brought my own sadness to a sharp point, and it had cut its way out of my mouth. Anyway, that's what I said.

Mike turned around and looked at me.

"Hey, man. Sorry," Easy said. "Rough."

Then Mike dropped down to the street again, and we all just sat there together, not talking.

• • •

After a while, I realized we were sitting smack-dab in the middle of Thornberry Lane. Old deserted shacks hunkered on all sides of us like dark night animals. There was just one light on the whole block, coming from the only inhabited house, Mrs. Beeson's.

In fact, the Toytaker's orange parlor lamp was burning not thirty yards away from us. Which goes to prove what desperation will lead you to sometimes. I, for one, wouldn't have been caught dead under ordinary circumstances loafing there at night. The neighborhood was creepy enough during the day.

But that night, you know, it was a funny thing. When I realized exactly where we were and fear began creeping into me, it almost felt good somehow. Fear began elbowing misery aside, and that was kind of a relief.

And then we saw headlights coming toward us. Mike must have thought they were his dad's lights, even though they were coming from the wrong direction.

"No!" he yelled, and he bolted from the street to the overgrown sidewalk.

We followed him, and all three of us crouched in the bushes till what turned out to be old Mr. Patterson's Chevy went inching past us.

We were directly in front of the Toytaker's house then, right up against the fence that held in her overgrown yard. From where we hid in the branches of a mulberry bush, we could see clearly into her parlor window, just like we were looking at a TV screen.

"Look at all that stuff she's got in there," Easy whispered in an awed-sounding voice, and Mike and I looked.

The room was shadowy with just the fireplace and the lamplight, but it looked crammed with all kinds of stuff—books and pictures stacked from floor to ceiling, feathers in huge old jars, about a million humongous plants that looked like they could have been man-eaters. And then Mrs. Beeson herself walked into the room, leaning on that colored walking stick, and went to stand in front of her fireplace.

"Let's get out of here," I whispered. But I was too frozen to move, and Mike and Easy didn't even act like they'd heard. Their eyes were glued to that window.

As we watched, Mrs. Beeson slowly raised her walking stick and held it in front of her face with both hands. It was weird.

And then a couple of her cats leapt onto the windowsill and batted at each other, and at just that moment we heard a pickup motor from down the road. Easy moved out of the bush, stood up and looked toward the pickup sound.

"Your dad, Mike," he said. "We better let him know we're here. You gotta face him sometime."

One of the cats fell off the window, and the other one jumped after it.

Mike and I moved back from the mulberry branches and stood up, looking toward the headlights. I went to stand by Easy, to help him edge Mike along. But Mike glued his eyes quickly back on the window, still stubborn about coming completely out of hiding. His face looked red and puffy in the lamplight.

And then something very strange happened.

"Whoa!" Mike said suddenly. The sound came out of him like he'd been kicked in the stomach. "Whoa!"

Easy and I both looked at the window then. Mrs. Beeson was still standing in front of the fire, in the same position as before.

But in her hands, instead of her walking stick, she held a brilliantly colored snake.

It was writhing in the air, wrapping its neck around one of her scrawny wrists as she cackled with delight.

•Eleven•

Well, we all ran then, of course. I mean, if you catch a witch in action, you run for your life. No ifs, ands, or buts about it.

We ran back out into the street, and Easy raised his arms to flag Mike's dad down. The headlights stopped in front of us, and we all three scrambled to get into the cab.

Easy, the last one in, slammed the door and locked it, then rolled up the window.

"Let's get out of here, Dad. She's a witch," Mike tried to explain, though he sounded like there was no air left in his body. "Mrs. Beeson. She's a witch. She just turned her walking stick into a snake."

I guess I thought maybe Mike's dad would crack up at that, would punch Mike's arm and wrestle him around.

But he just quietly drove to the end of that block, then pulled the truck over and parked it. He shut off the motor and turned to face Mike eye-to-eye.

"Listen, son, there's some things it's time you put

aside," he said, taking hold of Mike's shoulder with one of his big hands. "I just tried to tell you back at the pasture that there's no cowboys in Cloverton, and you ran from that like a scared rabbit. Well, son, there's no witches either. Understand? It's time you grew up enough to live in the world as it really is, not like you want to make believe it is."

"But Dad, I saw . . ." Mike started to protest.

Easy and I were hunched down in the seat, staring at our feet.

Mike's dad suddenly jerked his hand away from Mike's shoulder and brought his fist down hard on the steering wheel. It was the first time I'd ever seen him do such a thing—he was usually so nice and funny.

Then he took a couple of deep breaths, rubbed his eyes, and turned back to Mike.

"I need for you to be a man for me now, son," he said solemnly. "Our family is going through some rough times, and it may get even rougher. This old world is complicated and hard sometimes, Mike. I just need for you to understand the situation and face up to it and be a man, do you understand me?"

Mike didn't answer. Easy and I stared harder at our feet.

"Answer me, Mike. Do you understand?"

"I guess," Mike muttered.

But all the way back to unload the horse tank, Mike sat slumped down and sulking. And nobody talked at all when we got there. We just got to work, then went home.

I didn't have any trouble sneaking back up the trellis and into my room. My house looked dark and quiet, just the way I'd left it.

• • •

When I woke up the next morning, both my little sisters were sitting on the rug in the middle of my room, staring at me with their thumbs in their mouths.

"Our tummies are hungry," Cassie complained. "That old peanut butter you made us eat last night was rotten to the core."

Everything Cassie doesn't like is "rotten to the core." Everything she likes is "out of this universe."

"Isn't Mom up?" I asked, holding my breath. If she was up, then things would probably be all right. Once, though, my father had gone and stayed away for a whole week, and Mom went to bed and just stayed there. After three days of that, Aunt Caroline moved in with us to help out.

"Search me," Cassie said. But she said it quietly, without her usual bossy tone, and she looked like she was having a hard time keeping from crying. I understood then that she was still too scared to go in our mother's room.

"I'll check," I said, stooping to jerk her hair and wink at her as I crossed the room. Then I went down the hall real quick, so I wouldn't chicken out myself.

"Mom?" I pushed open the door a little and saw her bent over the ironing board, her back to me. She was in her orange terrycloth robe, her hair tangling across the back. She was barefoot, though the wood floors felt sort of cold to me.

She turned slowly and stared at me for a few seconds, her eyes dull. Then she just turned back around, like I didn't exist.

"Go away, son," she said. She moved the iron back and forth across something that looked like a dress. "Go take care of your sisters."

I closed the door quietly, feeling all hollowed out, and returned to where Cassie and Mame were waiting for me.

• • •

About an hour later I had the girls dressed and found some breakfast stuff for them and then cleaned up after that. There was still no sound of Mom moving out of her room. And I couldn't face going up there again to get further instructions.

So I decided to just leave a note in the kitchen and to take my sisters with me to Waco's pasture. I put them in the big wagon and pulled them all the way, with Sparky doing wild circles all around us.

When we got there, Easy was sitting in the grass, leaning against the trailer. He had a set of markers and a bunch of pieces of notebook paper spread out all around him.

"Hi, Teej. I been making up some plans for this place," he said.

Cassie scrambled out of the wagon when she caught sight of the jungle picture on the side of the trailer.

"Oh, that's just out of this universe!" she cried happily, running toward it. Mame tumbled out of the wagon and began half toddling, half crawling after her, laughing.

Easy grinned at them, and reached one long arm out to tickle Cassie as she ran up near him and started slapping her hands on the painted rhinos and elephants.

"Sorry," I muttered. "I'm babysitting today. I guess I better not stay long. Is Mike here yet?"

"Not yet," Easy said, standing up and swinging Mame between his legs. Easy's good with little kids. "I thought maybe he was coming out with you."

I shook my head. And then we heard the sound of bike tires on gravel, and Easy squinted.

"There he comes now," he said, and I turned to see him, too, a block or so away.

"I wonder if . . . you know," Easy said. "I wonder if he and his dad sort of made things up last night."

But as Mike drew near us, then bumped his bike across the ditch and jumped off to walk it the last few yards, you could read the answer to that on his face.

"Hey, Mike, the horse tank looks great sitting here by the trailer, don't you think?" Easy said to him.

Mike didn't answer. He just sort of threw his bike to the ground as though kickstands hadn't been invented yet.

"My dad left this morning to go to that stupid job in Tulsa," he said, his voice husky.

Then he just stood there, kicking hard at a big half-buried rock. He glared at the rock, and wouldn't look up at the tank or at us.

Well, I'd been holding things together pretty well, I thought, up to that point. I mean, I'd managed not to let my mother or my gone father or my crying sisters get to me, at least not all the way.

But Mike's rotten mood triggered all kinds of gloomy feelings in me, too. I started looking for a rock myself, which is not so hard a thing to find in the Ozarks. And when I found one, I started glaring and kicking, too.

Easy folded his arms and looked from Mike to me and back to Mike again. "Hey, snap out of it, okay, you guys? We got lots of work to do to get this place going! We've got to haul more water from the stream for these fish. Then we've got shelves and cages to build, and storage containers to rig up, and then there's . . ."

Mike and I looked up at him. Easy's enthusiasm was seeping into us, bringing back the excitement we'd felt yesterday, making plans out here. When Easy started walking over to the cage designs he'd been drawing, Mike and I followed.

"One thing, though," I said solemnly as we crouched to study Easy's careful drawings. "It's gonna be great working on this. But let's work together, okay? I mean, let's just stick together when we're out here."

I figured they'd know what I was getting at. The

Toytaker's shack on Thornberry Lane wasn't that far down the road.

"Right. We've got a pact, and we work together," Easy said solemnly. "Brothers of the Jungle."

Mike didn't answer, but he joined in when we raised our hands in the air, and slapped them together, hard.

• Twelve •

The summer moved into high gear after that. Mike and Easy went right to work on the Junglerama. I had to stay home with my sisters for a few days, but by the end of that week my dad still wasn't back and Aunt Caroline moved in with us to take care of Mame and Cassie.

The weeks of June hustled by as we gathered up scraps of wood and leftover nails from anybody we could get to give them up. We all found some good stuff in our garages and tool sheds, and the lumberyard men downtown chipped in some, too. Judd had a huge pile of rusty chicken wire in a back corner of the Emporium, which he let us have. We spent one whole week straightening that and steel-wooling it clean.

We all three had lawns to mow, and we decided to pool what we could save out of our mowing money and keep it to use when we eventually took the Junglerama on the road. We got an empty peanut butter jar and labeled it JUNGLERAMA TRAVELING

FUND and starting putting dimes and quarters into it. We chose to keep it at my house because I didn't have turkeys or a big sister to mess with it.

● ● ●

By the last week in June, every square inch of space inside the trailer was filled with shelves and secure cages and food cans, with only a small walkway left down the middle. And the fish were growing and thriving in the horse tank right outside. In my closet I had an old ten-gallon aquarium with just one small crack near the top, and we installed that in the trailer, too, to use for tadpoles.

Mike's mother gave us a gallon of bright gold paint that she bought to paint her bathroom with but then decided was too gaudy. We painted the outside of the trailer with it, all except the jungle picture, of course. The gold practically glowed in the dark, and it was the perfect flashy color to bring the jungle picture totally to life.

Judd gave us a big barrel with FINEST IN POULTRY FOODS printed across the side. We kept our personal supplies in that—sleeping bags, sweat shirts, markers, chips and candy, a couple of balls, a Frisbee and a few other things.

The day we hammered in the last nail and used up the last of the paint, the three of us spent an hour or so just sitting under the big cottonwood tree, trying to let everything sink in. It seemed incredible to us that we'd accomplished so much. The Junglerama looked like a solid gold nugget sitting there, shining in the sun.

None of us said anything for a long time. And when Easy Jack finally broke the silence, his words seemed very impressive. Like a poem or a prayer or something.

"Tomorrow," he said, "we hunt."

• • •

We took an old butterfly net of Easy's, a bucket that Mike brought, a couple of cardboard boxes, and some string and stale donuts. And we went back to the forest behind the Junglerama.

We caught three turtles back there our first day out—two red-ears and one small snapper that nicked Mike's tennis shoe toe as he nudged him into a box.

The stream that ran through the woods was alive with crawdads, tiny nearly transparent babies darting from place to place and big granddaddies sheltered under rocks with their pinchers sticking out. We picked a few of the red and turquoise granddaddies to keep and caught them with the butterfly net. We also brought back a gallon jar of tadpoles and put them in the aquarium, which we filled partway with rocks to make a neat frog nursery.

That same afternoon, while Easy and I were settling the crawdads into the old aquarium, Mike called from outside, his voice really urgent.

"Bring the net, you guys! Quick!"

Easy and I rushed out to see Mike pointing excitedly toward the shadows on the side of the trailer.

"Skinks!" Easy whispered. "The net, Teej, quick!"

I saw the tiny lizards then too, and quickly slapped

the butterfly net over three of them sunning themselves.

"Got 'em!" Mike cried. "Way to go, Teej!"

Half an hour later we had the skinks settled in a cage. The longest one wasn't more than four inches from his darting tongue to the tip of his tail. They looked exactly like dinosaurs caught in a shrinking machine. In fact, in my head I was already calling the longest, and angry, one *Tyrannosaurus rex,* Rex for short. Rex stood glaring at the three of us, belligerently flicking his tiny tail and his tongue while the other two lizards munched happily on dead beetles we'd given them from our cans of stockpiled animal food.

I didn't think anything could be as great as those skinks, but the next morning Judd and Easy were feeding the birds at the Emporium when they noticed a bunch of chickens frantically pecking at something. They chased them away to find a nest of baby garter snakes. The mother had already been killed trying to defend her young, and most of the babies hadn't survived the eager beaks of the chickens either. But there were four six-inch-long babies left alive and squirming in panic.

Judd lifted them with a shovel and put them in a cardboard box. Then he walked clear out to the Junglerama with Easy, and gave us careful instructions.

"I wouldn't hold with caging any snakes for too long," Judd told us. "Snakes have minds of their own and don't hold with bars. But if you boys have got a snake nursery out here, these little fellers could stand some watching over just now. Feed 'em some live earthworms and they'll truly love you forever, I reckon."

We put the tiny snakes in a large cage with window screen all around it. It was the only cage we had with mesh tiny enough to keep them in. The little striped snakes explored their new territory, then knotted together into a comfortable pile to take a midmorning nap, looking totally content.

From his cage across the aisle, Rex glared at them suspiciously, his head tilted to one side.

• • •

The next afternoon we decided to make another trip into the forest, this time to wade the stream, looking. We kept our tennis shoes on for grip as we crossed the large moss-covered limestone rocks that made up most of the stream's bottom. We used big sticks for balance.

Easy led the way, Mike followed, and I brought up the rear. We headed downstream. The water got really deep in places, up to our chests. And the current was pretty strong. The shadows through the trees got longer and longer, stretched finally clear across the water as the afternoon got late. And it seemed like the longer the shadows got, the quieter it got in the woods.

The back of my neck was starting to feel tight, and I kept thinking I saw creepy things out the corner of my eye, hiding in the trees. I started to wonder why

Easy didn't turn around and start back. I kept remembering this movie I saw where these guys were rafting a river and crocodiles came out at night and ripped them to shreds.

Then suddenly, Mike froze. He was about twenty feet in front of me, and he just froze stock-still.

"Huh?" I asked, whispering, stopping too with my heart thudding. "Huh, Mike?"

He raised one arm and pointed down into the water. His face looked white.

I tried to get my own legs to rush to help him. But in that movie anybody who tried to help the guys the crocodiles were gnawing only ended up eaten themselves.

Easy, though, turned around and hurried back toward him.

"Be careful, Ease!" Mike croaked out then. I could tell from his voice, which was full of fear but not pain, that he was still in one piece, at least. That was something.

Then Easy was just a few feet from him, and he took his stick staff and pushed it into the water like a spear. A couple of seconds later he raised it out, and the most horrible monster I had ever seen was hanging onto the end of it by his jaws.

He was big—about a foot and a half long, at least. He had four stubby legs that were pawing the air angrily, and he looked like loose, walking slime. His face was broad and flat, and his eyes stared straight out from each side of his head.

"Hey, it's a hellbender! Wow, come here, Teej,

and see this!" Easy cried. "It's a salamander, Mike.
Not really dangerous unless you stick your finger
close enough for him to think it's a worm. I saw one
once when it bit on Judd's fishing line and he pulled
it to the bank. He nearly had a heart attack. They're
not poisonous, but they sure are super ugly."

The awful walking slime that Easy had called a
hellbender let go of the stick then, and fell into the
water. I went splashing and tripping for the shore
before I really thought about what I was doing.
When I reached the safety of the muddy bank, I
looked back and saw Easy and Mike staring at me.

"What you doing, Teej?" Mike called over to me.

I tried to think of something fast.

"I thought it might come this way," I said, feeling a
little queasy. "I . . . planned to catch it for the
Junglerama."

Mike put his hands on his hips and cocked his head
to one side, squinting up his eyes at me.

But Easy shook his head with a smile.

"Wouldn't be a good idea, Teej. We made a pact to
be true to the spirit of the jungle, and that means not
trapping anything that's not going to be happy in captivity. And that guy would have been miserable."

I flopped down on my stomach, relieved that at
least Easy had believed me and hadn't thought I was
afraid. I was pretty sure I hadn't fooled Mike, but it
looked like he was going to drop the subject anyway.
A couple of minutes later, Mike and Easy waded to
the bank and lay down on the stones beside me. I

turned over on my back to watch the sun leak into the clearing the stream made.

"This is great," Mike said after a couple of minutes when the only sound was the water. "You know what I wish? I wish we could stay here and in the Junglerama all the time, and never had to go home at all."

"Ummm," Easy agreed.

"Right," I said. "But I guess we're not as lucky as jungle animals. We do have to go home, no matter how miserable we are in captivity."

• • •

Maybe I shouldn't have said that.

Because it seems like it was right then, at that exact second, that everything changed. One second we were lying there in the sun, free and happy. And the next, afternoon was changing to early night and the wind felt clammy on our bare chests.

One second we were in the forest, resting and letting our minds drift.

And the next second we all knew we had to rush upstream through the cold dangerous water, toward home, and that we would be late and in trouble when we got there.

"We better go back. It's going to be getting dark," Easy said suddenly, jumping to his feet.

So we trudged back through the water, across the soybean field, and finally got near the trailer. And something a lot worse than I could have imagined was waiting for us. Or at least, for me.

•Thirteen•

Sparky had gone to the woods with us that afternoon, but when he saw our plan was to wade in the water, he changed his mind and headed back to the trailer. I figured he'd chase rabbits for a while, and end up zonked out under the cottonwood tree. So I was really surprised when he came bounding to meet us as we returned to the Junglerama, whining in the back of his throat.

"What is it, boy?" I asked, and he looked at me out the corners of his eyes, shivering. That look clearly said "Brace yourself and don't say I didn't warn you."

Easy and Mike both frowned and squinted toward where the sunset was flashing off the gold paint of the Junglerama.

"Looks the same," Easy said, but his voice had an edge of suspicion to it.

The three of us kind of shifted into a sneak walk then, more stealthy and quiet than before. Sparky got behind us and scooted through the soybeans on his stomach, trying to hide behind his floppy ears.

When we got a few yards from the back of the trailer we all stopped and listened. Nothing. No sound, not even wind.

Then Easy took the lead, and I hurried to get close behind him. We snuck around the side of the trailer, hardly breathing. My system in that kind of situation is to hold my hands out in a karate position, which I did. I also stuck my neck down into my T-shirt in case we were about to deal with a slasher, like that guy with the razor fingernails.

"Nothing," Easy said, standing right by the door of the Junglerama, scanning the road up and down in both directions. "All clear."

We all let out our breath with relief.

"What happened, Spark? Did you chase something that turned tail and chased back?" Mike teased him.

Sparky just gave him an insulted look, then stared at the door of the trailer, starting up that throat whine again.

We all immediately tensed up, and Mike and I looked at Easy. Something was in there, in the Junglerama itself.

After a few seconds, Easy cleared his throat. "We better go on in and feed the animals," he said in a not-quite-normal voice. He stepped up the little metal stair under the door, then Mike and I followed him.

And I think we all three saw it at practically the same instant.

A long, bright red snake with white and black rings on his coat was writhing and gliding inside one of the biggest cages, near the snake nursery. A tag had been fastened to the cage, lettered with green crayon, which you could read clear from the doorway.

"'For you, boys,'" Mike read while we all stood paralyzed. "'From Mrs. Cora Beeson.'"

"It's . . . it's . . . ," I said, but my mouth wouldn't work right.

". . . the snake we saw her make from her staff," Mike finished in a husky whisper.

"Copperhead?" I asked, my throat so dry that my voice went squeaky on the last syllable. The colors were right for a copperhead, one of the most poisonous snakes in Missouri. But I couldn't remember how the stripes were supposed to be.

"No," Easy whispered. "Just a red milk snake. Not poisonous. But . . . but . . ."

It was the first time I could remember Easy being rattled enough not to finish something he started to say. I looked at him, and I was pretty sure those old voodoo drums were pounding in his head.

And boy, if even Easy was scared, you better believe I was plenty well scared, too.

"It's witched," I said, which I thought was pretty obvious. "So who cares if it's not poisonous? It might as well be. I knew she saw us watching that night. I knew we wouldn't get away without paying."

The snake quit gliding and jerked its head over to fix me with an icy look, hissing.

I sort of stumbled backward out of the trailer then, missing the metal step, which I had forgotten was there. I picked myself up and looked down the gravel road, where a car was racing noisily toward us in a cloud of dust. A few seconds later, Aunt Caroline skidded her Ford to a stop in front of me.

"Thomas, is Cassie with you?" she shouted from the open window while the road dust swirled in her face. She looked strange, hollow-eyed and scared, not heavy and calm like she usually looked.

"No, she was home with you when I left this morning," I told her, feeling like I was caught in a bad dream.

Aunt Caroline breathed heavily in and out once, then covered her eyes with both hands and drew in a shuddering breath.

"I was pretty sure she wasn't with you, but this was our last hope," she said. Her voice was shaking. "Get in the car, Thomas. Your sister has disappeared. Everybody in town is out looking for her. Your mother has gone completely to pieces."

I ran around to the other side of the car and jumped in. I glanced up to see Mike and Easy crowding the doorway of the trailer, looking at me. They looked as shaken up as I felt.

"We'll feed the animals quick and get into town to help look," Mike said in a rush.

I nodded.

"Hey, Teej? We'll find her," Easy said.

I nodded again, numbly, but I had the sickening feeling that we wouldn't.

All the way racing back to my house with Aunt Caroline, I clenched my jaws and crammed my fists hard into the hot plastic of the seat.

That snake of Mrs. Beeson's had fixed me with cold clammy eyes, hissing directly at me, zapping me with black magic.

Only a witch could have known how to curse me to the core. Only a witch would have thought of removing from the face of this earth my little sister, Cassie.

•Fourteen•

I tried to stay calm enough in the car so I could understand Aunt Caroline's explanation of what had happened.

She said she had left Cassie playing dolls on the front porch, and had run into the house to change Mame's diaper. She'd only been gone three, maybe four, minutes. But when she came back to the porch, Cassie and her three Barbies and all their clothes were gone. That in itself about proved witchcraft, as far as I was concerned. There was no way Cassie could carry all those Barbie things by herself, if she'd just wandered off. No way. And Aunt Caroline distinctly said there was no Barbie clothes trail leading from the porch.

No trail. No Cassie.

She'd just vanished, into thin air.

As we got close to our block of houses, you could tell everyone in the neighborhood was outside looking for her.

"Sheriff Perlman has a posse spreading through the

fields and the woods," Aunt Caroline said. Her voice sounded so dull and heavy that you would have thought her vocal cords were made of concrete. "We've searched all the buildings downtown, and now they're searching again. Everybody in town is helping, Thomas. Everybody is out there just tearing things to pieces, looking."

She pulled into the driveway and stopped the car. Then she turned to me, her eyes wet and shiny.

"So that means they'll find her, don't you think so? Wouldn't you say so, Thomas?"

I stared at her knuckles, where they clutched the steering wheel, shaking and white. I wanted to help her, but I couldn't answer the question she'd asked.

So I just got out my door, and started walking like a robot into the house. I went numbly up the stairs, into my mother's room.

She was lying on the bed on her back, one arm hanging limply over the side. Her mouth was open.

"Thomas, the doctor was here. I called him when your mother . . . well, when your mother needed some help," Aunt Caroline whispered from right behind me. "She had a little trouble today, handling the situation. The doctor gave her a shot to help her get some rest."

I turned, like a walking piece of wood would turn, whacking my shoulder on the doorway.

I walked on down the hall.

And when I passed the bathroom, I could tell something was funny. There was a pile of glass in the tub, and streams of gooey green and yellow ran down some of the walls.

"Your mother . . . your mother broke some shampoo bottles in here," Aunt Caroline said. "She just had to get out some of her panic, I think. When she threw those bottles against the wall, I'm sure she was only trying to throw some of the worry out of herself."

I kept on walking, one foot and then the other foot, down the hall. I could feel Aunt Caroline's eyes on my back, leaving two hot holes in my shirt. My sisters' room was dark, but I could see Mame's little chunky shape in her bed in there, alone. I jerked my eyes out of there and went on to my own room. Aunt Caroline followed me inside.

"I'm going to the woods to look for Cass," I told her. "Soon as Easy and Mike get here."

"No!"

That two-letter word, practically screamed, was the first thing that really cut through the curse-haze in my head. I jumped a little and looked at her, waiting.

"Please, Thomas, don't go out again tonight," she said real fast, coming over to me and taking my arms in her hands. "I just can't handle this any longer today alone here, with just the baby and your mother the way she is. Can you understand?"

I thought back to the two million or so times I'd been really afraid in my life, and I could tell that was what poor Aunt Caroline was feeling right now. The kind of fear that eats into your guts.

"Sure," I said.

And she pulled at me and smashed me against her and hugged me hard and cried. And I just stood there and let her.

• • •

So I stayed home and spent most of the night sitting on the floor by my window, looking out at the street and hoping against hope Cassie would come wandering back, dragging those Barbies by the hair. And then I pushed open the screen and laid out on the porch roof and listened close to the night, wishing I'd hear her voice, or that smacking sound she made when she sucked her thumb.

Then I guess I dozed a little, and finally the black sky turned a little bit light.

• • •

I discovered the electricity was off when I crawled back through the window at dawn and tried to turn on the light by my bed. Nothing. I looked back out the window and saw the houses across the street looked dark, too. No streetlights, nothing.

I'd promised Aunt Caroline to stay in the night before, but this was another day, and I couldn't wait to get outside, looking for Cass. So I tiptoed down the hall, checking real quick to see that everybody was still asleep. Mame was a small lump under her covers, Mom was lying exactly like she had been the night before, and Aunt Caroline was sitting and snoring in the chair beside her bed. I tiptoed into Mom's room just long enough to check and see that she was still breathing. Then I went on down the stairs and out the front door so quietly even Sparky didn't wake up.

Since the clocks in the house were electric and weren't working at the moment, I didn't know what time it was. But I figured it was almost light enough to call it morning, so I decided to stop by and get Mike.

When I knocked on his door, Molly answered. Past her shoulder, I could see Mike and his mom sitting at the kitchen table, a candle giving them some light.

Mike's mother hurried over to the door, and pulled me inside by the wrist. "Come on in, T.J. Have you had breakfast? Sit. Eat."

I followed her over to the table, and noticed that Mike looked strange, kind of worried.

"Hi, Teej," he mumbled, then just kept smashing his cornflakes quietly into the milk with his spoon.

"Oh, T.J., I was just talking to Molly and Mike about how I think this is a job for the state police," Mike's mother said. "Your sister's disappearance, I mean, and now the lights going off like this. It's just . . . it's just so strange, so nerve-wracking."

I could see now why Mike looked worried. His mother was talking too much and too fast—she was usually so quiet and calm. While she talked, she got up and brought me a bowl and glass from the cupboard, and when she put them on the table I saw her hands were shaking. When she turned to get the juice, Mike and Molly frowned at each other, then looked quickly normal when she came back.

"I'm just . . . just so sorry for your mother, T.J.," she said then. "When something like this happens it makes you realize . . . makes you realize how important it is for families to be . . . together."

Then suddenly she put her hands over her eyes and pressed them there for a minute. Her chin began quivering, and she got up and threw her napkin on her chair.

"Oh, dear, I'm so sorry," she whispered, and went quickly from the kitchen. A few seconds later we heard her shut her bedroom door.

Molly sat looking at her plate for a few seconds, then she wadded up her napkin and threw it at the refrigerator.

"Everything is just so awful this summer, in this awful hot trailer with Daddy gone!" She sobbed. "So awful. And now who knows who, or what, is out there, just waiting for us? Why can't Daddy be here?"

Then she, too, ran down the hall, and we heard her door bang closed.

Mike looked at me and shrugged.

"My mom's pretty upset," he said. "So's my sister."

I nodded.

Mike got up and went over to where his Cardinals hat lay on the coffee table. He picked it up and fished in the lining, and brought out a crumpled slip of paper.

"My dad gave me this a month ago, the night before he left for Tulsa," he said. "Actually, he just left it in my room. It's the phone number of that place where he's shoveling out those horse barns. I think I'm supposed to call him if some emergency comes up or something."

I'd just put a spoonful of cornflakes in my mouth, but suddenly they felt like nails and I couldn't swallow them. My dad had been gone a month, too. Only who knew what his phone number was? I sure didn't.

"Even if I called him and he came home he probably couldn't do anything to make my mom and sister feel better," Mike mumbled hoarsely. "If he can't even keep farming or find a job cowboying, he's probably too much of a wimp to do anything about the bad stuff going on here."

It nearly choked me, but I swallowed the soggy mass of cornflakes in my mouth, and stood up. I walked over to Mike, feeling like my brain was cooking. I think it was that word "wimp" that did it.

I actually grabbed hold of his arm, just above the elbow. He looked surprised, but didn't jerk away.

"Hey, what makes you such an expert on wimpiness all the time, anyhow, huh, Mike?" I asked him, my eyes stinging. "'Cause, see, I don't think you even know how hard it is to just keep doing something, and doing it, and doing it when you'd rather just forget it and run away. Even if it's just plain drudge work, like taking care of sisters and then even having one witched that you can't even find. You have to just keep doing things sometimes, instead of yelling or escaping, no matter how hard or gross those things are. If I had your dad, I'd be real proud that he had the guts to stick around with your family and do something gross and hard like shoveling out those stalls. I'd say that took a whole bunch more courage than just doing something fun and flashy like cowboying."

I never in my whole life thought I'd ever talk to Mike like that. When I finished I was shaking all over. I let go of his arm, and he just left it sort of stuck out, like I was still holding it.

When I slammed out his door, he was standing like a statue and frowning, still holding his arm out like that.

•Fifteen•

I ran to the Emporium then, my blood pounding in my ears. I figured what I'd told Mike probably hadn't made much sense, and in a way I wished I'd kept my mouth shut. But in another way, whether what I'd said made sense or not, and whether Mike would ever speak to me again or not, I was glad I'd gotten it off my chest.

Easy was on his way out the big gate when I got near the Emporium, and he threw up one arm and waited for me.

"Any news?" he called.

I knew he meant about Cassie, and shook my head.

"I stayed up most of the night, checking and re-checking the cages," he told me as I approached. "I just kept hoping Cassie might have gone exploring in one of them, and fallen asleep inside or something. You know how she liked the birds, whenever you brought her out here, Teej?"

"*Likes* the birds," I whispered, and my throat burned. "Don't talk like she's . . . she's . . ."

"Hey, Teej, I'm sorry," Easy said quietly. "Hey, don't go to pieces now, man, all right? I know we'll find her safe and sound. We've just got to keep our heads together and stay cool."

I had to breathe deep and really concentrate before I could talk right.

"But the thing is, you know as well as I do it's a curse," I whispered. "There's nothing we can do against it."

Easy didn't answer. After a couple of minutes, he put his hand on my shoulder, and we walked in silence the rest of the way downtown.

• • •

When we got to Main Street, there wasn't any sign of Sheriff Perlman or a posse. But a crowd of several old men was gathered right outside the Tip Top Bar, and Judd was one of them. They were just standing on the sidewalk, swaying and looking up into the sky as if trying to figure out if what they saw up there was for real.

As we got close to them, we squinted through the gray light and saw their attention was focused on the thick, black overhead wires leading into the town's small electric power plant, which was in a square concrete building between the bar and the post office.

Easy followed their gaze up to the wires, and when I saw the expression in his eyes I was almost afraid to look.

But then I did look, and what I saw made me feel more than ever like we were trapped inside some bad dream or horror movie or something.

Four small snakes and one larger one were wrapped around the wires.

They were limp, electrocuted. Their deaths must have caused the electricity to short out, leaving the town without power.

"Oh, no," I heard Easy say. "It's them. Ours."

I'd realized that too. I could see from the stripes down the sides of the small snakes that they were the baby garters from the Junglerama. I could see the brilliant markings of the large snake, and knew it was the red milk snake Mrs. Beeson had left us.

The one that had carried the curse.

My heart was thudding in my ears. Or maybe the jungle pounding of the voodoo drums was so strong in Easy's head that it was dribbling into me.

Neither of us moved a muscle. We just kept standing there, mouths open in shock, staring up. And then I suddenly realized the sun was getting hot. Some time had passed and a big crowd had gathered around us and Judd and his friends.

In fact, that crowd included Mike. He was standing on Easy's other side now. I glanced over at him cautiously, sure he'd be mad. But he just seemed as confused and flustered seeing me as I felt seeing him.

"I called my dad," he mouthed across Easy, his hands like a megaphone around his mouth. I frowned and shrugged, not able to understand very well over the growing murmur of the crowd. He edged behind Easy, squeezed through to stand by me. "I called my dad, Teej," he said, his voice fast and excited. "He said . . ." He stopped and swallowed a few times, looking down. Then he raised his head, took a deep breath, and looked me in the eye.

"Teej, my dad said he's coming home tonight. And he said I acted like a man, calling him. A man, Teej. Those were his exact words, 'like a man.'"

And then, before either of us could say anything else, everybody was suddenly talking at once in loud, hissing whispers. Sheriff Perlman's patrol car had just pulled to the curb. The sheriff quickly shoved his way to the front of the crowd with two of his deputies.

"What you plan to do about this, Sheriff?" asked a gruff voice, and it was followed by half a dozen echoes. An angry murmur was rising from the mob of people.

"We got a kidnapper on the loose, and now this . . . this obscene hocus-pocus with snakes!" shouted someone else. "It just ain't natural! It just ain't right."

Kidnapper. The word zoomed like a bottle rocket into my brain. Kidnapper?

I grabbed Mike and Easy by the backs of their T-shirts and started backing out of the crowd, pulling them along with me.

"What?" Mike asked, jerking out of my grip when we were back a few yards away from the action.

"Didn't you hear Mr. Houston, Mike? He said we've got a kidnapper on the loose! It was that curse Mrs. Beeson put on us with her snake that got Cassie. It wasn't any . . . any kidnapper."

They were quiet and looked thoughtful for a few seconds, then Easy took a deep breath and rubbed his forehead.

"Well, if that's what really happened, it would be

called a hex, not a curse. When someone leaves a gift that brings evil with it, it's called a hex."

"Fine," I agreed. "Just so we all know the truth and don't get off the track with that 'kidnapper' garbage."

Mike toed the sidewalk and shook his head.

"I don't know, Teej. I just don't know."

And then Easy was shaking his head, too, and folding his arms across his chest.

"Yeah, T.J. We all thought we saw her witch that snake. And we all know she left it at the Junglerama. Anything else, we still gotta prove."

Prove? What did he mean by that? How could we prove any of this?

But the noise of the crowd got suddenly louder, and all three of us looked over to see what was happening.

"Now, folks, what we don't need here is panic," Sheriff Perlman was saying, his hands out in front of him like he was pushing back something dangerous but invisible. "We'll find the little girl, and we'll most likely find how those animals got up on those wires too, if we all keep calm and work together."

But the crowd only became louder. And then Jacob Heims, Matt's father, stepped forward, his fist raised in the air.

"Sheriff, I'll say what some people's wanting to but ain't got the nerve," he shouted. "I say there's unnatural goin's-on here and have been for some time! Why, just look around us! The town's gone downhill, the big meat-packing factory closed last month, and now we got missing children and this . . . this ungodly mess today!"

He stopped and looked, grimacing, toward the power line. I saw then that he looked almost exactly like Matt, especially when he sort of snarled like that.

"I say lots of us know who, or what's, at the bottom of this!" he went on. "Lots of us don't need to look no further for the source of our troubles than that old place out to Thornberry Lane!"

The crowd grew suddenly quiet, then a few murmurs started up again. Sheriff Perlman just kept shaking his head. His shiny shoes were scuffed and dusty, and his shoulders were slumped.

"Jacob, I warn you and your friends," he finally said. But he sounded more beat down than forceful. "Don't take things into your own hands."

He began leading his deputies away, and the crowd parted for them.

When the sheriff had gone, most of the other people began to drift away, too. But Matt's father and a few of his cronies stayed, and we heard their angry talk as we moved forward to get Judd.

We couldn't make out their words, but we could tell they were making plans from the way they gestured, poking at the air with sharp finger jabs.

• • •

We didn't talk while we helped Easy take Judd home. We just thought, separately, about what to do next.

When we got inside the gate of the Emporium and near to the house, Easy tried to prepare us a little.

"Uh, I better stay with Judd till he gets asleep, and you guys can come in and wait if you want. Judd and I let the turkeys out into the yard, and we're going to start cleaning up the place, after I get back from helping look for Cass."

Then he turned the doorknob with his free hand, the one that wasn't bracing up Judd, and kicked open the kitchen door.

Mike and I hadn't been inside the house since the turkeys were hatched a couple of months before, and it was kind of a shock, to put it mildly. There were feather-covered newspapers and globs of turkey food everywhere, including on the chair Easy led Judd to and deposited him in.

"T.J., I'll bet Jackie here wishes he had some other kind of uncle for himself," Judd said when he saw me looking at things. "Yes sirree, I'll just bet he does."

Easy brought the big aluminum trash can from the kitchen and began shoving some of the papers from the floor into it. Mike and I bent to help.

"Uncle Judd, I'm on to you, you hear?" Easy laughed as he worked. "I know you're just trying to get us to feel sorry for you so you won't have to push a mop so hard this afternoon when we really tackle this job."

But Judd just repeated himself, more softly and sadly.

"Yes, I'd say you got yourself one poor excuse for an uncle, Jackie boy. Smart, fine boy like you ought to have better, and that's a fact. Well, maybe you won't have old Judd to worry with much longer."

Easy straightened up suddenly, a wet and goopy

section of the Sunday comics forgotten in his hand. He looked different than I'd ever seen him look. Not sad exactly, or angry, or even afraid. Just—different.

And then it dawned on me. Easy looked at that moment exactly like I felt every time I thought of Cassie, lost and alone somewhere. Easy looked helpless, and a combination of those other three things—sad, angry, and afraid.

"Uncle Judd, you quit talking so crazy now," he said, forcing another laugh.

But Judd had fallen asleep, slumped in that filthy chair, snoring lightly with his mouth sagged open. He looked awful—yellowish, and skinnier than I'd ever seen him.

"He's drinking way too much," Easy whispered, staring down at Judd. "He's wandering too far in the damp night air, and he's looking old and sick beyond his years."

Then he looked from Judd to Mike and me, his eyes bright and sad.

"I can't imagine life without Judd," he said. "It makes me feel all empty inside."

Thinking of Cass, I put a hand on Easy's shoulder, then Easy ran a hand across his eyes quickly, shot me a half smile, and bent back to work.

• • •

We helped pick up the last of the turkey papers, then left Judd sleeping at the Emporium, and went out to feed the animals at the Junglerama. It was the last thing we had to do before we could begin seriously searching for Cassie.

At first we just walked along the dusty road to the Junglerama in silence, kicking at gravel. Then finally Mike opened up the subject that was on all our minds.

"See, what I can't understand is, why does Mrs. Beeson have it in for us?" he asked. "I mean, assuming she did hex us and that caused Cassie to disappear. Why'd she hate us enough to do that?"

I couldn't believe Mike had already forgotten all the stuff we'd figured out about the Toytaker that first year she'd moved to town!

"Hey, Mike, don't you remember?" I reminded him. "'Toytaker, Toytaker, Zombie, Ghost, and Ghoulmaker'? Don't you remember when we figured out that she grabbed toys mostly so she could lure little kids? Probably she hexed us just because she wanted Cassie, or she could have hexed us just for the fun of it. You act like a witch needs a logical reason, or something."

Easy looked from one to the other of us, but didn't say anything for quite a while. When he finally did speak, what he had to say made my bones feel flimsy as river mud.

"Mrs. Beeson walks by the Emporium a lot at night," he said. "And lots of times she stops, just stops and stares through the fence. The way she walks like that at night and stands and stares, the way she gave us the snake. Well, if it's truly a hex animal, then I suppose we should consider the possibility that she could be a zombie, raised from the grave to cause destruction."

After Easy dropped that bombshell, what was there left to say? So we all just walked, sneaking looks over our shoulders every few feet, until twenty minutes later we reached the Junglerama.

We fed the animals, and sadly closed the open door of the snakes' nursery cage. The big cage the milk snake had been in was open and empty, too, of course. But everything else looked just like we'd left it the day before.

There was nothing else to do out there, so we stood in the gravel road, thinking about our next move.

"I guess . . . I guess I just feel like there's only one real way to get to the bottom of this," Mike said, gulping. "We're the ones who owned the garter snakes, we're the ones Mrs. Beeson gave the milk snake to, and especially we're the ones who sort of own Cassie. I mean, we're like her protectors, right?"

He glanced at me when he said that, and I nodded hard. I liked to think of it that way.

"Right," Easy said, taking a deep breath and blowing it out. "So we gotta do it. Our next step is to go to Thornberry Lane to look for some clue to Cassie's disappearance at Mrs. Beeson's house. We're all mixed up in this and we've got to do what we've got to do."

Once Easy said it, we all knew it had been our only course of action all along.

•Sixteen•

We all went home then, to eat lunch and check in. But we met back at the Junglerama at 2:00, then started for Mrs. Beeson's. I brought Sparky back with me, and you could tell he knew something was up. As Mike, Easy, and I followed the gravel road in the direction of Thornberry Lane, instead of prancing along ahead like he usually did, Sparky hung back and walked at our heels, nearly tripping one or the other of us every few feet.

We hardly noticed that, though. We had too much else on our minds. I kept telling myself to keep my brain clear, not to think of any of the horror movies I'd seen, or the afternoon under the trailer. Or the staff-turned-snake. Or the cackle Mrs. Beeson gave us near the Haunted Palace. "So you like to be afraid, heh, boys?" *Heh, heh, heh.*

The more I thought about not thinking about those things, the more I thought about them.

When we reached the edge of town and started up the meandering lane of old shacks, I felt my stomach clenching and my feet started to feel like they might turn and run without my permission. Boy, if that happened in front of Mike, today of all days, I'd never live it down.

"Scared?" I whispered to Easy.

He shrugged, but I noticed he couldn't force a smile.

"There's worse things than fear," he finally said.

But at the moment I couldn't think of any, and he didn't suggest any either.

Then we reached the fence that held back Mrs. Beeson's garden. We were standing in almost the exact place we'd crouched the night Mike ran from his dad.

"Well, let's go in," Mike said.

Easy pushed at the latch on the gate. It was rusty, but it opened easily.

• • •

It looked like there had once been a pathway of bricks leading to the front porch of the house, but the bricks had been broken up by weeds and grass and tree roots into little red chunks. Still, only the area of red-chunked dirt was free of the tall flowers and weeds and stuff that clogged the front yard. We walked up that chunky pathway in single file—Easy, then me, then Mike—kind of like reluctant explorers on safari.

We were right at the bottom porch step when Easy stopped so quickly I walked right into his back.

"Ease!" I whisper-yelled. But then I looked around his shoulder, and felt the rest of my words freeze like popsicles in my lungs.

The Toytaker, Mrs. Beeson, was sitting on the porch, mere inches from us. She was rocking in an old willow rocker, both feet on the floor, wearing one blue sock and one red one. A huge yellow cat was in her lap, and another perched on the top of the rocker, its tail stringing down and around her bent, bony neck.

She was looking right at us with eyes like black holes.

"Well, well. Come to thank me for the snake I left you as a gift, boys?"

Her voice was full of ancient shadowy winds, like the stream behind the Junglerama, running out of its underground cave. Her wide smile seemed carved out of her wrinkled face. I felt all the blood in my body, every speck of it, fall heavily to my feet.

Mrs. Beeson stood up then and began a slow shuffle toward us, never lifting her feet, just skating them along. Cats I hadn't noticed at first fell from her in all directions. Then she suddenly stopped by the stairs and clapped her hands, like she'd remembered something exciting. She leaned toward Easy, and I cowered farther behind his broad back.

"Say, boy, do you know how I got all these cats?" she whispered, lowering herself to sit on the top step. Her black eyes had sparkles in them then.

"Uh, we better. . . ," Easy began, stepping back so that I stepped back quickly, too.

But behind us the gate slammed suddenly shut. I felt Mike jump behind me, and Easy drew in his breath.

"Well, it was like this," she said, speaking to the

calico kitten hanging by its claws from her hem. "One day as I was working in my garden, I pricked my finger on a yellow rose, and my blood ran out gold. Gold, mind you! Not yellow. Not that ugly orangish color they put in crayon boxes and call gold. But gold, gold! I went to the kitchen to get a silver cup to keep the drops in, and what should be there but a tiny bird. Perched on the back of my breakfast chair, he was! Well, he flew out the window presently, but later that day a box of chocolate-covered cherries came in my mail."

She jerked her head up, moving her gaze like a laser beam from the kitten to Easy.

"Explain that, boy, except that the bird brought the luck of it! You can't explain it otherwise, can you? Well, can you?"

"No, ma'am," Easy whispered.

I found myself moving a little to the side to hear better.

"Yes, well, I didn't think you could," Mrs. Beeson said, smoothing her skirt over her knees with a self-satisfied nod. For a couple of minutes she just sat there winding a long strand of her wild hair around one finger, humming to herself. She seemed to have completely forgotten about her story.

"And then another day," she said suddenly, "I was sitting in my breakfast chair having a chocolate-covered cherry, when I looked up onto the wall and found the word UNTIL written out with shadows. Now that's not something you see every day of the year, is it, boy? Well, is it now?"

I nearly choked. She was looking right at me this time!

"Uh, no, ma'am," I croaked out, swallowing hard.

"No, of course it isn't. So I ran into the cellar to get my camera out of the apple bin. And when I came back up, the shadows were gone, but there was a tiny kitten with orange fur sitting on the window ledge, just below where they'd been. And when I say orange I don't mean that washed-out orange they give you in *el cheapo* paintboxes these days. I mean jack-o'-lantern orange, boys! I named her Esmerelda, of course, and she was the mother or grandmother or great-grandmother of all the cats I have today."

Nobody said anything for a few seconds then. Easy and Mike and I just stood rooted there like her plants. And Mrs. Beeson rocked lightly back and forth on the step, humming and looking contentedly through her crammed-full front yard.

Then she sighed and stood—slowly, creakily. She turned and went slowly toward her door, then opened it and stepped through. Once inside her dark house, she turned slowly back around and held the screen door open.

"Well, what are you waiting for?" she asked us. "Come on in."

• • •

Mrs. Beeson scuttled down a tiny hallway, and disappeared into the cluttered parlor room Easy and Mike and I had peered at that night from under the mulberry bush. It was so gloomy inside the house that we stood in the hallway for a few seconds squinting, trying to adjust our eyes to the light. Trying to adjust our brains, too, to actually being inside a real haunted house.

Then we began groping our way into the parlor, past the stacks of books and baskets, and the clutter of cat dishes on the floor, past the reaching fern-arms of the huge plants.

Mrs. Beeson had reached the back of the house by the time we got halfway through the parlor, and she called to us from the doorway.

"Oh, but what's become of the other one?"

For a second, I couldn't figure out what she meant, and my heart banged with all sorts of horrible possibilities. The other ghost, monster, zombie? But then she went hurrying back past us, to where Sparky had his face pressed forlornly against her screen door.

"There he is!" she said, chuckling and opening the door for him. As far as I could remember, this was the first time in history Sparky had been let inside anyone's actual house. Sparky immediately assumed a haughty attitude, and would barely look at Easy and Mike and me as he followed Mrs. Beeson happily past us, to what must have been the kitchen at the back of the house.

"Sparky likes her," Mike whispered in my ear.

"That's doesn't mean anything," I whispered back. "She let him in, after all. He'd like anybody who did that."

We could see better now that our eyes were adjusted, and we looked around the parlor in astonishment. A telescope poked like a giant finger at the one big window in the room. Baskets and buckets of dried flowers were everywhere, some with cats sleeping in them. Instead of a rug, someone had painted a big smiling banana in the middle of the floor in front of the fireplace.

The room didn't smell too good. There were too many cat boxes in the corners for that.

"Well, come on back, boys, and have a chocolate-covered cherry!" Mrs. Beeson's voice came from the kitchen, and we could also hear the excited thump, thump, thump of Sparky's stumpy tail on the linoleum.

The kitchen was very bright. One whole wall was windows that looked out over the back yard and its tangled vines and fruit trees. Mrs. Beeson was sitting in an orange plastic chair pulled up to a rickety card table when we went in the room, with Sparky smacking his lips eagerly at her knees.

"*Hee-hee,*" she was saying, patting his head. I could see from the empty candy papers on the floor that he was going on his third chocolate-covered cherry.

"I can tell you love my home," Mrs. Beeson said to us, her eyes sparkling. "I could see you especially appreciated the moon picture I painted personally by hand on the parlor floor."

None of us could think of anything to say.

"The night I first walked by and saw your wonderful Junglerama, I knew you boys would feel right at home in my little place," she said to Sparky. "Isn't it so much more fun to be in a jungle of possibilities than in a tidy place where everything is set just so? I knew you four would understand. That's why I took you the beautiful snake I found in my garden as a housewarming gift, as a matter of fact!"

I was just beginning to feel relaxed a little and not quite so scared, when it suddenly hit me that that would be the worst possible thing to do. I'd seen this movie once where the aliens disguised themselves as nice ordinary people so they could lure the earthlings into a false sense of security, and then they got them in their rocket ship and slaughtered all of them and ate them.

"Uh . . . my sister has disappeared," I forced out of my dry mouth.

I couldn't believe I'd done it, that I'd actually brought up the subject of Cassie. Easy and Mike couldn't either, evidently. They turned to stare at me like I'd lost my marbles. Well, maybe they could be lured and then eaten, but it was my sister hidden somewhere in this house! My Cassie!

I think we all three held our breaths then, expecting something horrible to happen. Maybe Mrs. Beeson would cackle loudly, which would bring her fake cats to monstrous life, and they would shed their cat disguises and surround us and tell us Cassie was a goner and now so were we. Or maybe the floor would fall out from under us and we would slide into a secret chamber where Cassie and the other kids were kept (kids that everyone just assumed had moved away). Or maybe Mrs. Beeson would raise her arms and suddenly we would hear Cassie scream from the attic, where she was being guarded and tortured by the ghost of Jeremiah Harlan.

But none of that happened.

Instead, Mrs. Beeson only closed her eyes and made fists of her hands, and then brought them back hard against her bony chest. A tiny sound came out of her open mouth—a sad little "uh" of shock.

"How well I know the heart's ache of a disappearance!" she whispered then, her eyes still closed, her voice nearly a moan.

Easy reached out a hand to fiddle with the empty candy wrappers lying crumpled all over the table. Mrs. Beeson must have practically lived on chocolate-covered cherries.

"Uh, well, we thought you might have . . . seen her," he said finally, then gulped.

Sometimes I've wished Easy wasn't quite so brave. I mean, it was probably foolhardy enough for me to have told her my sister had disappeared. But this was really pressing things. I closed my eyes and waited for the worst to happen.

But Mrs. Beeson didn't seem to even realize Easy had spoken. Her eyes opened slowly, and her voice became high and cracked as she stared into space, remembering.

"It was my original cat Esmerelda's great-grandson, once removed. And I had named him Pumpernickel, of course, seeing as how he had the orange coat of his great-grandma but the silver eyes of a nickel. And that orange coat, if you'll recall, was jack-o'-lantern orange. And those eyes, well, a nickel is not really silver, but the color is silver, you see. That's what I meant."

Sparky gave a big bored snort. Mrs. Beeson ignored him, caught up in her story.

"And it was an October evening that Pumpernickel, that little darling of my heart, just disappeared. Disappeared! And oh, didn't I look for him? And I went to bed that night with a stone in my heart, having counted my cats seven times, and found him missing after every one of them. Well, and that next day I sat on the porch and I looked for his return. The trees were losing their leaves. The yard was filled with orange maple leaves. I sat on the porch with those leaves falling on me like plaster from the ceiling and I watched for him, and I watched."

She looked so sad by then that Sparky put his head on her knee, and she patted him absentmindedly.

"He . . . he never came back, then?" Mike finally prodded.

She jumped slightly, and looked at Mike like he had said the stupidest thing in the world.

"Why, of course he didn't come back!" She chuckled. "How could he when he never was gone to begin with! You get it, don't you? That little Pumpernickel had been asleep on a leaf pile the whole time! The exact color of those leaves, he was! Camouflaged, he was! I was looking at leaves when I looked at those leaves. I should have been looking for a cat asleep in the leaves, though, you see? You've got to see more than just the thing before your nose in life, and that's a fact."

Mike and I both stared. Easy squinted, and crossed his arms.

"Then you're telling us you think T.J.'s sister could be sort of like your cat, lost in plain sight?" he asked.

Mrs. Beeson sent a stream of giggles like bubbles into the air, as she rummaged through the cherry box, crinkling papers, exploring.

"Could be, boys," she said, licking chocolate off one thumb. "All I say is a person looking for something lost has to take the trouble to see everything there is to see, no matter how hard that is. Why do you think I use that telescope in there instead of my poor old eyes? To see the whole sky and everything in it, that's why! The big picture, boys. Learning to see the big picture, that's the ticket."

Suddenly, Sparky caught the scent of a rabbit or some other animal in the dense undergrowth just outside the house, and he barked and dashed to the kitchen screen door. Before we knew what was happening, he'd squeezed through a cat hole in the bottom of the screen and disappeared completely in the tangle that was Mrs. Beeson's back yard.

"Where'd he go?" I hurried to the door, but I couldn't see any trace of him. I felt panic flood over me.

"Through the tunnel, most likely," said Mrs. Beeson, pointing to where the vines and branches formed a sort of passageway to the alley far out back. "He's discovered the secret entrance! I used to use it all the time, but in years of late it's become too over-grown for those of us who are larger than a cat or dog."

She sighed at the unfairness of that situation.

Something about seeing Sparky virtually disappear that way had broken the spell we'd been in, and I think we all three were suddenly scared again. We were in the kitchen of a probable witch, after all!

"We better go out the front way and catch up with Spark," Easy said quickly. "He'll probably head back for the Junglerama once he's through pestering that rabbit he smells."

And we grabbed that excuse to hurry back through the house, out the front door, and down the path to the gate. To our relief, it opened for us when we pushed against it.

"Thanks for the candy!" Mike called over his shoulder.

"Yeah, thanks!" Easy and I echoed.

The last glance I got of her, Mrs. Beeson stood in the shadows just inside her door, leaning on that walking stick of hers and watching us go.

•Seventeen•

We ran hard all the way back to the Junglerama. I felt like I'd been choking down a huge dose of fear all the time we'd been in the Toytaker's house, and now it was turning to pure speed as it hit my legs.

"What do you think?" Mike puffed as we neared Waco's pasture.

Easy slowed, his hands on his waist, panting.

"She talks kind of crazy, but actually she seems pretty nice," he said when he had enough breath back. "Sparky sure does like her."

I couldn't believe she'd taken them in like that, with a few chocolate-covered cherries and a couple of stories!

"But you guys, her walking stick! We saw her turn it into that snake, remember?" I asked them.

Easy shrugged, shaking his head. "I don't know. I just don't know, Teej. She said she found the snake in her garden."

Mike frowned and slitted his eyes, concentrating.

"And you know, I was the only one of the three of

us actually looking at her window then, remember?" he said, pulling on his lip. "You guys were standing up then, looking down the street toward my dad's pickup. I called you guys to see when the snake was in her hands. And, well, I was pretty upset. And there were cats jumping around on the windowsill and everything . . ."

"Are you saying you guys are doubting now that she's a witch?" I asked, my voice sort of squeaky with disbelief. "Then how do you explain the snakes this morning? If it wasn't witchcraft or voodoo or something that made them fly up around those wires like that, then what was it?"

Nobody answered. We were about to the pasture gate by then, and Easy reached out to lift the latch. It was then we heard something strange. It was a scared sound, sort of like a low, frightened moaning, and it was coming from inside the Junglerama. Automatically, all three of us began moving in slow motion, tiptoeing toward the door.

"Please!" came a voice from inside. "Oh, please, just let me out and I won't bother you, I promise!"

"It sounds like . . ." Easy whispered.

"Carl Tyler!" I finished for him.

Mike nodded in agreement, and the three of us rushed the last few yards to the trailer and burst in practically on top of each other.

Carl was standing with his back against the wall farthest from the door, his arms outspread and his legs wide apart, as though he wanted to flatten himself enough to totally disappear. The two red-eared turtles were wandering around on the counter near him, their cage standing open. Easy and Mike and I looked quickly around at the rest of the cages, and then we saw it.

The two small skinks were still in their cage, huddled contentedly near their water dish. But there was a wide place between two of the wires of the cage, big enough to be an escape hatch for a tiny four-inch-long lizard.

And Rex was standing in the middle of the floor, inches from Carl's ankle, hissing and threatening and waving his head belligerently in the air for all he was worth.

"Call him off!" Carl croaked when he saw us in the doorway. "Call off your vicious poison lizard before he climbs into my pants leg!"

Mike turned around quickly, biting the sides of his mouth to keep from laughing out loud. I felt giggles starting inside me, too, working their way up my throat. They felt good.

But Easy didn't act like he thought it was funny. "Sorry, Carl, there's no calling him off once he's got his prey cornered," he said solemnly.

That really cracked Mike up. He snorted, and I kicked backwards at him to shut him up.

"See, Carl," Easy continued, "we trained Rex to guard our snakes. They disappeared this morning somehow, and I guess that's what's got him riled."

The mass of giggles dissolved in my throat as I suddenly realized Easy wasn't joking around. He suspected something. Something bad. Mike got serious real quick then, too, and took a step toward Carl, his face white.

"It wasn't my fault!" Carl yelled. "It was Matt's idea to get 'em and throw 'em up there around those power lines like that! Daryl and I only helped!"

I just stood there, trying to get through my skull what Carl had just admitted to. But Mike jerked forward furiously and bent to snatch Rex up, then crouched there patting him to calm him.

"He's not poisonous, Carl," Mike spat out, looking up at Carl with anger steaming hot and blue from his eyes. "Rex wouldn't hurt a soul, unlike you and your pitiful friends."

I'd hardly ever seen Mike so mad. I was mad, too, but something else was tangling around in my head, something that seemed more important to try to sort out and understand.

Mrs. Beeson hadn't jinxed those snakes after all.

"Calm down, Mike," Easy was saying, though I hardly heard him through my own thinking. Carl took advantage of that moment to shove past all three of us. Outside he ran for town without looking back.

Easy kicked the door once in hard frustration, and Mike was breathing hard, still pale.

Magic hadn't caused the death of the snakes. I tried to comprehend that and what it meant in terms of Cassie. Maybe it should have made me feel a little better to know it.

But as I looked at those empty cages, for some reason my fear for Cassie kicked up another sickening notch inside me.

"I'd better be getting home to check on Judd and help muck out that mess inside the house," Easy said after a while. "I'll meet you guys tomorrow. We've got that mowing job, remember? Then we'll look some more for Cass if she hasn't come home."

He gave me a steady look, then finished quietly. "But Teej, I'll just bet she turns up safe at home by then."

"I better get home, too, to be there for when Dad gets in," Mike said. "You coming, T.J.?"

I looked at the empty cages again, then raised my eyes to look out the little side window of the trailer, toward the woods in the distance.

"I think I'll hang around here a little longer," I said, pushing the words out my dry throat.

Those woods were just waiting there, with afternoon shadows leaking out. A witch doesn't need a logical reason to cause harm, and we'd just seen with our own eyes that some people don't need one either. That was the thing. I shivered, realizing for the first time it wasn't just witching we had to worry about. Those woods could wrap any horror—magic or man-made—in their seeping shadows.

I had to do it.

I had to walk out the door of the Junglerama, walk through the soybean field, and look back there along the creek. That part of the countryside probably hadn't been combed as thoroughly as most other parts. After all the animal hunting we'd done back there, I knew that stretch of woods inside out. I knew every shallow cave, every bend of the creek.

Mike and Easy left. When they were out of sight, I went out of the trailer and turned and started into the woods, which were getting darker by the minute.

I should go back there and see. I should go right now. I told my feet to start moving.

But I suddenly knew my plan was a dud because I just couldn't do it, couldn't face that rushing water and the sound of scampering, hidden things, human or otherwise. I just couldn't go back there by myself, all alone.

I flopped down against the bank of the road, grabbed two handfuls of grass and threw them angrily at my feet.

"You big wimp! You big wimp, you big chicken!" I grabbed my hair till it hurt real good. "You ought to be ashamed. You ought to be the dog hiding there under the trailer, and Sparky ought to be the person! You know that? You know that? You ought to be the chicken in one of Judd's cages and that chicken ought to be out here in your stupid human skin!"

I jumped to my feet and whirled angrily in the road, kicked the ground till gravel bounced up and stung my arms.

I was boiling mad at myself, and tears were pouring from my eyes and making me even madder. I rubbed my eyes and my nose till my face was plastered with gunk, then I faced the creek again, hoping my misery would make me brave somehow.

But for the life of me, I knew I couldn't go into those woods alone.

Instead, I ran back toward town, toward home. I

was so ashamed that I actually believed if there was any justice in the world I would be turned into a dog, or a chicken, at any second.

• • •

When I got home I was pretty much a miserable blob, without thoughts. My mother was sleeping again or still. My aunt was ironing in the kitchen.

"Thomas, Dr. Salvers was here and gave your mother another shot," Aunt Caroline said. She looked tired and her voice was flat and heavy. "He says she'll sleep the rest of today, and will probably feel a little calmer by tomorrow."

"Oh," I said. My eyes had fastened themselves to the crayon picture Cass had made of our family a couple of weeks before. It was attached with a carrot magnet and a smiling frog magnet to the refrigerator. Dad was in it, too. My stomach started aching.

"I'm going to my room, okay?" I said, and headed for the hall.

"Thomas, don't you want a sandwich or something?" Aunt Caroline called as I was halfway up the stairs. I pretended not to hear.

• • •

I spent the next hour or so lying on the floor with my legs up on my bed, bouncing a tennis ball against the wall. Pretty soon Mame toddled into the room and lay down on her stomach beside me, sucking her thumb.

"Cassie gone, T.J.," she said every few minutes.

Every time I bounced the ball it meant a tiny speck of time had gone by, which was a little bit of a relief at least. Then suddenly, for some reason, I remembered that it was July third, and that made me remember the firecrackers. Easy and Mike and I had spent a few dollars from the traveling fund for them the week before. We had stored them in the supply barrel outside the Junglerama, and now I probably wouldn't even get to help shoot them off.

The second I thought that, I also thought that I made my own self sick to my stomach, even thinking about firecrackers at such a time.

I slammed the ball against the wall so hard a chip of paint came loose.

"Cassie gone now, T.J.?" Mame said.

"Cassie's gone, but we'll find her. Don't worry, okay?"

I could hardly force those words out of my throat.

"Cassie gone, T.J."

I turned to look at Mame. Her face was about three inches from mine. Her eyes were nearly closed. I reached out and wiped the sweaty, sticky orange hair from her cheek.

"We'll find her, okay?"

My arm was too tired to throw anymore. I let the ball roll away under my bed, folded my arms under my head, and lay there staring at the ceiling, trying to pretend I wasn't anywhere.

•Eighteen•

I guess I fell asleep like that. The next thing I knew it was dark in my room, and Mame was gone. There was a sandwich for me on a plate on the floor by my elbow. I got up and walked down the hall and saw Mame was asleep in her crib, and the clock by her bunny nightlight said 10:37. Mom's door was shut, and I figured Aunt Caroline was sacked out either in there or on the couch.

I went back to my own room and shoved some blankets and the sandwich plate out the window, and crawled out after them. If I slept on the roof I figured my head would be clearer and I could think some things through. I spread out the blankets and flopped on top of them, balancing the sandwich on my stomach.

I heard a few firecrackers go off in the distance. Nothing like you would normally hear the night before the Fourth, though. I guess the mothers of the town had put the lid on fireworks noise, out of respect for my mother and because they didn't want their kids out after dark, with something out there ready to nab them, like Cass had been nabbed.

Okay, that was it. The main thing I had to think through.

Did the Toytaker nab Cass?

Suddenly, a thought slammed into my head.

"Her staff!" I whispered to myself out there on the roof. "She still had it when she stood in the doorway, watching us leave her house! How could she still have it, if she turned it into that snake she gave us?"

Okay. I had to put this together, to see the big picture. Witch or not, that "big picture" thing Mrs. Beeson had told us made a lot of sense to me.

The parts of the picture, counting everything I could think of, were—Cassie gone, the dead snakes shorting out the power, the meat plant closing and so my dad leaving, farmers like Mike's dad going broke, Main Street being full of closed-down stores, Easy having voodoo drums pounding in his head, Judd drinking too much and wandering around at night and looking sicker and sicker. Did all that add up to witchcraft? Was it part of a pattern that started when the Toytaker moved to town and that was coming to a gruesome head this summer? Was that the big picture, all there was to see?

Suddenly, a hot dry wind came up, the kind of wind people dread on the Fourth of July, a wind that can take a single spark and set a cornfield blazing with it.

I anchored my blankets down harder with my

heels and elbows, and tried to figure out why I suddenly had such a creepy feeling. A feeling that tomorrow would bring something bad our way.

The big elm tree began tossing like a groping hand above my head, and I could hear the tire swing thunking against its trunk like something dead and mutilated. The sandwich flew from my stomach and went flapping into the darkness.

I got under the blankets, including my head. And just as I began to swirl down into sleep I thought I heard the tapping of the Toytaker, as she roamed through the hot, windy night.

• • •

I woke up about dawn, stuffed my blankets back through the window, and climbed in after them. Like Easy had reminded us the afternoon before, he and Mike and I had a big mowing job that morning. We had a deal with the Town Council to mow the park for the fireworks display that night. When we'd landed the job back in June, we'd been real excited, thinking about the big chunk of money it would be for the Junglerama traveling fund.

Now, though, I wondered if the deal was still even on. Would the town have the fireworks display this year, or was everyone too busy looking for Cassie? Too busy, and too upset to celebrate?

I tiptoed past my sleeping family, down the stairs. By the time I got to the kitchen, I'd been in my house long enough for the walls to start closing in on me, like they had all the time since Cassie had been gone. I realized that fireworks display or no fireworks display, mowing the park this morning would be something solid to do.

So I wrote a note telling Aunt Caroline where I would be, and I dragged the mower out of the tool shed. Sparky stood slurping his tongue around, begging me to take him.

"Okay, but don't blame me if it hurts your ears," I told him.

Then we escaped, to the park.

After a couple of dozen pulls on the cord, the lawn mower sprang into smoky action. Sparky went running away from it, tail stub between his legs, as usual. It still wasn't completely light out, and for a couple of seconds I wondered if I was going to be waking anybody up in any of the houses ringing the park. But then I realized it was too late to worry about it—if they weren't awake by now after a few seconds of our mower's wild, sputtering noise and smoke, it would take a barrage of grenades to wake them.

The park is big, shaped like a circle around a lagoon. I was on my third pass around it when I looked up and saw Easy coming, pulling his mower. He started in on the opposite edge from me, so I narrowed my tracks to take half the space. A little later Mike showed up, and each of us adjusted to a third—a fat wedge of grass like lime pie, ending in an imaginary point in the center of the lagoon.

Our system on a huge, shared mowing job like that is to grit our teeth and work, without breaks or anything. It's too hard to start again if you once stop on a hot day.

So that's what we did that morning. Just kept on chugging till the job was done. When I finally ran out of grass, the sun was directly over our heads. I looked over and saw Mike had just finished, too, and Easy was waiting for us at the bandstand. Mike and I went toward him. The quiet hurt my ears when I switched off my mower.

"Whew," Mike said. "Hot."

Easy nodded from where he slouched on one step of the bright white-painted stand.

"Looking good, though," he said, scanning the entire park.

It did look good, a lot better short like that.

"Lemonade at my house. My trailer, I mean," said Mike, already turning to lead the way. His house is the closest one to the park. We followed him, suddenly too thirsty to stand it.

• • •

"To Wasserville," Molly said when we burst in the door and headed for Mike's refrigerator.

We drank a quart of lemonade we found there, passing it between us. Molly just stood nearby, rolling her eyes in disgust.

"Where'd Mom and Dad go?" Mike asked then, wiping his face with the edge of his T-shirt and putting the empty pitcher in the sink.

"I just told you, fritobrain! To Wasserville," she answered. "And don't bother asking me why. Because I don't know, and even if I did they would have told me not to tell you because you always get your hopes up way too high."

"I do not!" Mike whirled around from the sink, his hands on his hips, fuming.

"You do so," Molly continued, so sweetly I figured Mike wanted to pop her one. "Why else would you go ahead and win nine fish when you live in a zero-fish trailer? You're just always hoping things will be like before, like in our old house. And Mom and Daddy don't want you getting your hopes up now, just because Daddy heard about this job managing the hardware store right down the highway in Wasserville. That store where he used to shop all the time for farm tools and things. And just because when Daddy called about it this morning, the guy remembered him and sounded all excited and told him to come right over and talk about it, even though it is a holiday. And just because Mom says there's a chance we may even be able to buy our old house back—just the house, not the land—because she heard those new people are sick of putting up with the plumbing and might sell it dirt cheap."

I looked over at Mike. His mouth was partway open and his eyes bulged. I wasn't sure he was breathing.

Then he turned and punched the air and charged outside, nearly going right through the door when it didn't immediately open. He jumped over the railing of the porch stairs, landing practically on top of Sparky.

"Now remember, Mike! I didn't tell you!" Molly called out to him. "And besides, I just said it might happen, not that it will!"

Easy and I rushed outside, too, then, and waited for Mike and Sparky to quit running around the yard, yelling and jumping and yapping like maniacs.

Molly stood behind us, shaking her head and rolling her eyes. But when I glanced back at her, I could see she was smiling, just a little.

"Oh, no, Mike. You don't get your hopes up. Not you," she said softly.

•Nineteen•

Mike hadn't shown any signs of coming back down to earth by the time Easy and I left a few minutes later. At the corner of Mike's block, where Easy and I would have to split up to go in opposite directions, I sat down on my mower.

"What's wrong, Teej?" Easy asked, crouching beside me like I'd hoped he would. "Aren't you going on home?"

My elbows were propped on my knees so my arms made a circle out in front of me. I stared through it at where some ants were running around in a crack of the sidewalk. I could have squashed about thirty or forty of them with one whack of my shoe, before they knew what hit them. And all of them would probably have had brothers left at home, and mothers and possibly even fathers.

"Where is she, Ease?" I whispered. "Just, where is she anyway?"

My eyes burned and my throat felt like I was being

strangled. I thought to myself I would never, ever do anything like squashing ants again.

"Hey, man," Easy said. "The posse's still out there, looking. People in town are looking. And you and Mike and I will keep looking. When I get home I'm going to search all through the birds' sheds and the woods behind the Emporium again. It'll be all right. You'll see, okay?"

I shook my head angrily.

"Looks like Mike's gonna have everything again," I muttered, then felt ashamed.

But Easy seemed to understand what I'd meant, and didn't hold that comment against me. He just rubbed Sparky, who was lying sympathetically on my feet, then lightly punched my shoulder.

"I'll bet by the time we meet tonight at the park, she'll be home," he said softly. Then he stood and started off toward the Emporium, dragging his mower behind him.

I watched him leave, wishing I'd had the nerve to ask him to come with me to search the woods behind the Junglerama. But then I would have had to admit to him I was scared to go back there alone, and even Easy might not have accepted that when it concerned my very own sister.

• • •

When I reached my house, I shoved the mower back in the shed, kicked the door shut, and dragged myself up the porch stairs. Sparky dropped into his hollowed-out sleeping place in the dirt under the porch, beat.

I figured Aunt Caroline would be in the kitchen getting lunch or something. I didn't know if I felt rotten from the heat and mowing all morning after not much sleep, or from all the worrying. But I sure did dread having to talk like a normal person with her.

But I was in for a shock. Aunt Caroline was no-where around, and my mother was sitting there at the table when I walked in the kitchen door. Her long nightgown was up and twisted around her knees, and she held a slipper in one hand. She was just sitting there, staring at the wall in front of her.

"Mom?"

She turned her eyes to me, then her whole head, too. Slowly, slowly. She squinted, as though trying to figure out exactly who I was. Then she opened her arms wide.

"Come here," she said.

I went to her, and she hugged me for a long time. She was soft and scared, and I felt kind of more like the parent than the kid. I patted her back, feeling clumsy.

"It's okay, Mom. It'll be okay. I know it will," I told her. Then things started sort of letting go inside of me, like they had when I was a little kid and she hugged onto me.

"T.J.? Oh, T.J., what are we going to do?" she asked me then, her voice breathy sounding, like wind. Her eyes looked scared and sort of swimmy. I figured those sleep shots from yesterday were still working on her a little, making her sort of dopey.

"It's okay, Mom. Don't worry, okay?"

That's what Easy had just told me. Now, telling it to her, I believed it a little more, for some reason.

"Son? I . . . I haven't ever told you. That is, I want to tell you now. You're my rock, Thomas. My rock, with the girls, with things around the house here, now that your father is gone. I depend on you. You're my rock."

And then her chin started shaking and her eyes got all glazed, and she slumped in her chair, sobbing.

I stood looking down at her, letting her words sink into my skull. I was her rock? I couldn't believe it. She depended on me? *Me?*

A funny thing happened then. I went and got a paper towel for her to cry into, and while I walked across the kitchen linoleum I started feeling my blood going through my body. I started feeling my muscles, and even my bones.

My mother hadn't hugged me like she had a few minutes ago since I was Mame's size. She was weak right now. She needed me. For the first time ever, I knew right then that I was strong. Strong as Mike, maybe, in my own way, strong as Easy, even.

"I'm going out to look again, Mom. I'll be back later," I told her.

• • •

And I went to the woods behind the Junglerama, alone.

When I got there, I was afraid. But there was something else riding on top of my fear, like a guy holding down and steering a skateboard. I thought of how strong and powerful all the animals in the Junglerama were, pushing through the air and water, moving fearlessly through their world. I concentrated on being like them, free and strong like that in my world.

It seemed like, now that I had the knack, by concentrating I could feel my muscles and bones anytime I wanted to. Several times that afternoon I tried to feel the separate parts of myself, alive and strong. And I found I could.

• • •

There was no trace of Cassie in the woods, though. By the time I'd searched everywhere along the creek in both directions, it was getting toward early evening. Easy and Mike and I had planned to meet at the park right before nightfall, so I headed in that direction.

There were lots of people when I got to the park, but you could tell it wasn't a normal Fourth. Instead of sitting around on the grass with coolers and picnic baskets, everybody was huddled near the bandstand, standing around and talking in whispers. It was obvious they expected someone to come and talk to them. Grown-ups were keeping their little kids close by, gripping small hands in their large ones. Some little toddlers, used to running free through the park, looked up at their worried parents and whimpered in frustration.

Easy and Mike were already there, sort of semi-hiding in a clump of cattails by the lagoon, back away from the rest of the people. I hurried over to join them, and at just that moment Sheriff Perlman pulled up in his squad car, even with the bandstand. His three deputies got out with him, and the crowd eagerly parted to make a path for them to the steps of the bandstand.

"When did you guys get here?" I asked, dropping into the reeds beside Mike and Ease.

"Just now," Mike answered. "I waited around for my parents to get back from Wasserville, and finally gave up and just left a note."

"I been here awhile, watching," Easy said, his eyes on the crowd by the bandstand. "Judd's been downtown drinking all afternoon."

"What do you think's going to happen?" I asked, speaking in a whisper for some reason. Nobody was within a hundred feet of us.

Easy shrugged and frowned.

"I don't know, man. From what I've seen, everybody in town is scared and upset, mostly about Cass. But I think they're throwing other things into their worry, too—the snakes, the bad luck the town's had here lately. I have a bad feeling about this. A bad feeling."

Yeah. So did I. The crowd was too tense, and the sheriff looked tired and discouraged. I remembered the elm tree scratching on the roof the night before, the hot wind blowing like a warning.

Sheriff Perlman had reached the stage of the bandstand. We couldn't hear all his words, from the distance we were, but we could tell from the way he was using his hands that he was trying to keep everyone calm. We kept hearing phrases like "keep our wits about us" and "work together without losing hope."

When he finally went back down the stairs and into his squad car, there was a smattering of applause for him. Most of the people seemed a little more relaxed.

And then, like a scorpion dashing from under a rotting log, Jacob Heims darted up the stairs, his wild gray hair flying in all directions. He was followed by three other guys who kept their heads ducked, kept staring at their boots. He waited only long enough for the sheriff to leave. And then, unlike Sheriff Perlman, Matt's father spoke angrily and plenty loud for us to hear even at our distance. He kept jabbing the air with his clenched fist.

"I grew up in this town, and I can't believe what I'm seeing here this week!" he yelled. "This used to be a community of real men and brave women, not a nest of lily-livered cowards! It's time we took things here into our own hands and cut out the cancer that's killing us all!"

Several people looked down at the ground and walked quickly away. A couple of women even put their hands over their kids' ears as they left. Lots of people were looking at Jacob Heims like you'd look at a two-headed cow.

But some few moved closer, as though eager to hear what he had to say.

"We all know in our souls what demon's got into our town! First she took our jobs and our farms, and now she's out to steal our very children! How else can a thinking man explain the run of miserable luck that's befallen us? The sheriff won't act against her because he's afeared. Well, me and my boys ain't afeared of nothin' that lives on Thornberry Lane, are we now, boys?"

The three guys behind him shook their heads, still staring at their feet. Two of them began grinning ear to ear.

"They're enjoying this," Mike whispered in disbelief. "I think they're actually enjoying Cassie being gone. Look at their faces—they're the center of attention, and they're lapping it up."

I felt something hot race through me. At first I thought it was fear, it was making my heart beat so fast. Then I realized it was anger. Anger at these men who valued Cass so little they could smile like that about her being gone.

Easy ran his hands over his face.

"I knew it," he said. "I knew something bad was headed our way. She's gonna need our help."

Mike and I looked quickly at Easy then, in surprise. What was he talking about? But Easy was staring intently at the bandstand, where Jacob was nearly in a frenzy now. Mike and I turned back to watch him, too.

"So I say we put an end to this and do it now, tonight!" Jacob yelled. He was so worked up that his face was wet with exertion and spit, and he wiped a tattooed arm across his mouth. "Anybody who's man enough will know where to be when the sun goes down. I guarantee me and my boys know where to be, and what to do, too! And we'll be carrying our rifles!"

And then he strode down the stairs, two at a time, with his three friends like overgrown puppies at his heels.

"Ease . . . Ease, what did you mean just now?" I asked quietly, although I guess I knew. "Who needs our help?"

"Hey, you guys heard!" Easy said in a rush. "You heard what they just said about rifles! Jacob's crazy enough, I imagine, to do just about anything to make the town think he's something. You know Matt—nothing's too mean for him to do, and I suppose he comes by that naturally from the look of things . . . It's Mrs. Beeson who needs help, and she needs it now!"

"But how can we . . ." Mike began.

"We can just get her away, out of that house of hers. Hide her for the night until this blows over a little," Easy said, squinting in thought.

"But what if . . . what if . . ."

The words had come from me.

I bit them off and felt my neck burning as I stared at the water of the lagoon.

"Say it, Teej." Easy was looking right at me.

I took a deep breath and met his eyes.

"Okay. What if she really is a . . . a witch?"

Easy and Mike were both quiet for a few seconds. Then Easy took a deep breath and let it out.

"Okay, it's time," he said. "Decision time for all of us."

We sat there in the tall grass by the water. The night sounds were getting loud—peepers in the lagoon, locusts and mosquitoes. There was a mist starting to rise from the water into the cooler air. Evidently there weren't going to be fireworks—everyone was going home, hurrying.

"Answer, guys. After what we've seen this week and this summer, do we think Mrs. Beeson is the one to be afraid of around here? Or is it just easier to be like Jacob? To blame one old lady for all the problems this town's got?"

Mike dropped his chin onto his hands.

"I think my dad was right," he said slowly. "We don't have cowboys in Cloverton, and we don't have witches. No heroes, no villains. Just a lot of people scared of the changes happening here."

I closed my eyes, took a deep breath, and tried to feel my bones and muscles. And I did feel myself, every molecule.

"Okay, then. Let's go," I said, surprising myself half to death.

I got to my feet and, for once, I was the one who led the way into the darkness, toward Thornberry Lane.

• Twenty •

When we got to the row of shacky houses that made up Thornberry Lane, things were even worse than we had feared. Around a dozen people were gathered in front of Mrs. Beeson's house. We could see them in the darkness because a couple of them carried kerosene lanterns. A couple of others carried rifles. They were milling around and making a droning sound like a hive of riled-up yellowjackets.

"Now what?" Mike asked. He sounded dried up, like somebody had packed sand into him. "We can't make it through that crowd. No way."

The house was dark, except for the oil lamp Mrs. Beeson always had burning at night in her parlor window.

"No, we can't. And if she's in there, she's in bad danger, that's for sure," Easy said.

And then all three of us thought of the same thing at the same second. Mike snapped his fingers.

"The tunnel!" we whispered together. Easy began running silently through the shadows, back the way we'd come, toward the jungley lot behind Mrs. Beeson's house. And Mike and I were right behind him.

It took us several minutes of combing the alley behind the house to find the overgrown opening of the tunnel. I kept wishing I'd woken Sparky and brought him with me—he would have known right where it was. When we finally found the opening, we ducked into it and crawled on our stomachs through the dense thicket of blackberries and wild roses. We felt our faces and hands being scratched, but still we tried to kick the vines into a wider opening—wide enough to lead Mrs. Beeson back through. We took out our pocket knives and carved away a thick grapevine that totally blocked the path for anyone higher than a dog.

It took us nearly half an hour to work our way to the back of the house. By then, we could hear the crowd becoming louder and angrier. We knew we had to hurry.

Crouching low, Easy made a run the ten feet from the end of the tunnel to the screen door leading into the kitchen. He crashed through the screen, widening the cat hole in it several inches in the process. Mike and I followed after him, and we all three landed on the kitchen floor and rolled.

"Mrs. Beeson?" Mike whisper-called, trying to be soft and loud at the same time.

There wasn't an answer. Not even a single cat was stirring.

Mike ran into the parlor, and Easy and I checked in the cellar.

She was in the attic, the place we all three searched last. She was covered with cats, sitting in an old chair with a broken rocker. She seemed to be just . . . waiting.

When we stuck our heads through the hole in the floor and saw her there, she turned slowly to us, stroking a huge cat. She smiled. The moonlight coming through the round attic window lit her face, made her eyes look like they were filled with dark jewels.

"Well, hello, boys," she said calmly. "Come for another chocolate-covered cherry? By the way, I'd like for you to meet Pumpernickel."

The ugly, cross-eyed tomcat rubbed his head under her chin as she looked lovingly down at him.

"Mrs. Beeson, quick!" Mike yelled, running to her. "We've got to get out of here!"

Easy hurried to her other side, and the two of them practically carried her to the opening in the floor and pushed her through while I held the trap-door open. Her cats slid around her as if they were magnetized to her feet.

When we reached the kitchen, we propelled Mrs. Beeson and her cat swarm out of the house and into the tunnel.

"Hurry, Mrs. Beeson! Hurry!" Mike hissed at her. The crowd was growing angrier, louder.

Easy went first, clearing the tunnel of vines that had tumbled since our other trip through. Mike went next, pushing along the cats. Then came Mrs. Beeson, and I brought up the rear. I tried to be a

167

cheering squad for Mrs. Beeson, and tried not to think of what might happen if that mob caught us and trapped us inside this dry tangle of weeds.

We'd be like caged rats, ripe for the slaughter.

"Hurry, Mrs. Beeson!" I whisper-yelled again.

"*Hee, hee, hee!* What fun, eh, boys?" she chortled just ahead of me.

The cats that slipped past Mike drifted all over us, like needles sewing us all together. One tiny calico rode on my back the whole way.

When we finally cleared the tunnel, we began running. Mike and I each held one of Mrs. Beeson's hands and pulled her along, and Easy came right behind us, herding kittens and cats.

"This is like flying!" Mrs. Beeson called, laughing. "Wheee! Like flying on a broomstick through the night!"

Easy and Mike both jerked around and looked at me when she said that, like they were worried about how I'd react. But something about it struck me funny, and I laughed out loud.

And then we were all laughing, laughing and running and leaving the milling crowd far behind in the night. By the time we reached the Junglerama, we were out of breath and slaphappy from all that running and laughing, and from relief.

But Easy, as usual, was planning.

"Listen, Mrs. Beeson," he said. "We've got sleeping bags and I can make you a nice bed inside the trailer. I'll spend the night outside here, guarding things, and by tomorrow that crowd around your house will probably have this out of its system and will leave you alone."

Mrs. Beeson chuckled, and bent to pick up an armful of cats. And when she straightened she was still smiling, but her smile was sad, there in the moonlight. It brought my own deep sadness galloping back—sadness about my gone father, my lost sister, my mother as broken-to-pieces as those shampoo bottles she'd crashed into the bathtub.

"Boys, those people outside my house—I've watched their like for a long time now," she said. "They have never learned in all their lives to see the big picture. They only have small eyes, eyes that see pain, suspicion, and fear. Eyes that will never be happy until they can learn to see the cat hidden in the leaves."

I thought of Cassie as she spoke, and of our useless search for her. I wanted to ask Mrs. Beeson if she thought we had seen the big picture where Cassie was concerned. Had we seen the cat in the leaves yet? Or when we chased all around the woods and the town and the countryside, were we only seeing the leaves?

In fact, I opened my mouth to ask just that.

But then I noticed that Mike and Easy and Mrs. Beeson were all staring wide-eyed and speechless into the night, down the gravel road. I looked, too, and what I saw made my insides freeze.

Orange tongues were licking at the black summer sky, snapping at a moon that hung like a disappointed face above the edge of Cloverton.

The town was on fire.

•Twenty-one•

"Oh." Mrs. Beeson's voice was a small explosion of pure sadness in the black night air. "Oh, my. Oh dear, dear."

It was her house, burning there in the not-too-far distance. Her house and everything around it. I glanced at Easy and saw his hands clench into fists as he watched the hungry flames gobbling everything on Thornberry Lane, then looking for more.

"Let's go check it out," Mike said quickly, starting forward. "Maybe we can help."

But Easy raised one hand.

"No," he said, stopping us in our tracks. "Not a good idea. I don't want to leave Mrs. Beeson unguarded. And do you realize how late it's getting? Your mothers will be really worried if you guys don't get home pretty quick, especially if they see the flames."

We knew he was right, of course. And even at this distance we could see lots of cars pulling up around the fire. Then the volunteer fire truck from Wasserville arrived, flashing and screeching. One trouble with being twelve is that people think you're in the way when there's big trouble, like a fire. The grown-ups were already coming out in gobs to help and probably wouldn't have let us anywhere near.

So reluctantly, Mike and I started home, walking backwards most of the way and watching the fire. When we got a few blocks away, Easy and Mrs. Beeson and the Junglerama were silhouetted against the flames like black cutouts against an orange piece of paper.

• • •

The kitchen clock said it was almost ten when I snuck into the house. I hoped everybody was asleep so I wouldn't be in trouble, and I was in luck. Aunt Caroline and Mame had fallen asleep curled up together on the couch, the TV still on. I turned off the television, covered them with the afghan and went upstairs. Mom was asleep in her room. I went on to my own room, and climbed out on the roof to watch the fire.

The flames were going strong. I could even hear the crackling and some shouting from the people trying to put them out. I kept imagining Easy, right over there near enough to feel it and smell it. He could stay at the Junglerama all night without even asking anybody, since Judd was probably out and wouldn't make it home till morning. Easy didn't have a bunch of family to tie him down and could do all kinds of neat stuff, that lucky.

The minute I thought that, my chest felt tight and my eyes burned.

I didn't mean it. I loved my family, all of them.
Even when they yelled.

But it just didn't seem fair sometimes that Easy
didn't have a father and so was free, and now I didn't
have a father but I was even less free than I used to
be. It didn't make sense. It was like you had to pay a
whole bunch for something, then you didn't get it
anyway.

Boy, did I miss my dad. That fact sailed into me
with an ache so pure it nearly doubled me over. My
dad, and my sister.

I turned my back on the fire and put my hands
behind my head and laid down on the porch, trying
to think of a different subject before that one
smothered me alive.

I decided to think of my plan, weeks that seemed
like years ago, to go to Florida or California to pitching camp. My dad always said we'd take a trip to
Florida someday. Who knew? Maybe he was there
right now.

I shut my eyes tighter. Was there any subject that
was safe? How about something rock bottom simple,
like breathing. I thought about breathing, breathing.
Just breathing the harsh sooty air.

It was then I heard the car driving slowly down our
street, even though cars practically never came down
our street that late at night. No, it was a truck. It had
that clattery engine most pickups in town did.

I sat partway up and looked down through the
elm branches to see if I could see it. Yes, there it
was, about a block away. Then suddenly it turned its

lights off, still driving down the middle of the road. Funny.

Funny.

I sat all the way up then, holding my breath. My blood was pounding in my ears.

The truck cut its engine, and just coasted down our block like a dark, silent ship.

Someway, I knew that truck was going to pull up and stop in front of our house, even before it did. And though it was too dark to see it clearly, something was making my throat close up and my legs feel like ginger ale as I looked down through the sharp elm leaves toward it.

The fire was a bright, glaring wall of sky to one side of the porch and back behind me. The street was a swirling mess of shadows on the other side of the porch, beneath me and in front of me. And inside those shadows, like a submarine in a midnight ocean, was the truck.

My eyes had trouble adjusting to the shadows after watching the fire. As I squinted downward, the door of the truck slowly and silently opened, a darker square of shadow reaching into the night. I stared, not daring to blink or breathe.

"Orange sky! Oh, that's just out of this universe!" came a high little voice from inside the cab of the truck.

Cassie!

I can't remember dashing across the porch roof or sliding down the trellis. I only remember hitting the ground and getting up and running and stumbling the last yards to the truck. If there had been a weirdo homicidal maniac driving, I would have rushed right into his waiting razornails, I guess. Because before I knew what I was doing I had thrown the door open wider and was sticking my head into the shadows, toward my sister's voice.

"Cassie! Cassie!" I laughed or cried or yelled.

And then I came to my senses enough to realize my sister was being held by, was leaning against, a larger shadowy shape. His arm was around her. But his eyes were on me.

"Son?" he said, his voice all husky and sort of scared-sounding.

"Dad . . . ," I choked out. "Dad."

"I was coming home, son," he said in that strange, husky voice. "I truly was, two days ago. I pulled up in front, but I just couldn't go in. I couldn't get up the nerve. And then I saw Cass, and she ran to me, and I couldn't let her go. I know when I took her it was a terrible thing, but I just couldn't . . . let all of you go."

He turned his eyes to the road, and I saw his jaw muscles working, in and out, in and out. Cassie patted his cheek and stuck her thumb in her mouth and scrambled across his lap, into my arms.

"Oh, you," I said, blowing raspberries on her neck, not letting her see my eyes. Her chunky, sticky little shape looked better to me than anything ever had. "Oh, you, Cass."

And then suddenly the lights came on in the house, right behind me. Dad jerked his face toward them, like he'd heard a shot, fear and dread dancing in his eyes. Sparky stumbled groggily out from under the porch, growling in the back of his throat.

"Dad?" I said.

I could see he was petrified at what was coming. I wanted to tell him I knew how he was feeling, that I knew a thing or two about fear and dread myself. I wanted to tell him to please, please face whatever he had to. If I'd learned to feel my strength this summer, then surely he could feel his right now, too. It would be worth it, for all our sakes. For my sake.

I couldn't think of words for that first stuff. But I did get across to him that last part, at least.

"Dad?" I said. "I need you to stay."

He tore his eyes from the lighted house against the burning sky, and planted them right onto me. He looked totally surprised, like he hadn't thought of that.

"You . . . do?" he said, and his look of shock turned to a sort of quivery smile. "Well, then."

He pulled himself out of the cab, shutting the door of the truck behind him with a solid chunk of sound.

I sort of half sat down and half collapsed on the grass with Cassie in my lap, and watched as he walked slowly toward the front door, alone.

• • •

The stuff that went on the rest of that night was grown-up stuff. To tell the truth, I understood only parts of it. But I mean, sometimes I seriously wonder if even grown-ups really understand how grown-ups think, or why they act like they sometimes act.

Anyway, first Dad talked to Aunt Caroline, then they woke Mom, and Dad talked to Mom. I could tell this from the way the lights went on in different parts of the house, though I stayed outside with Cassie. No yelling yet, I was very relieved to hear.

Then Mom came running out and grabbed onto Cass and kept crying and crying. But crying softly, into Cassie's hair. Still, no yelling, which I took as an extremely good sign. I saw my dad and Aunt Caroline waiting for us on the porch, so I put my arm around Mom's shoulders and led her back to the house.

"All right," Aunt Caroline pronounced when we were all on the porch. "T.J., you help me put Mame and Cassie to bed, and then the four of us will have a family conference, right here and now, around the kitchen table."

Aunt Caroline has been a schoolteacher up in Milwaukee for years and years, and when she starts in she can really get things organized.

"Family conference, you say?" Dad asked softly, glancing sideways at Mom. Mom just clutched Cassie tighter and didn't say anything. But I'd noticed her eyes on him, too, once in a while, sneaking over like quick fish.

"Yes, family conference. I hope both of you, Libby and George, realize how far things have gone this time. Too far, in other words. Libby has had what amounts to a nervous breakdown, and George, you have committed what amounts to kidnapping. And if you two don't make plans to get some professional help at this point, then I myself won't hesitate to call the authorities and get you some help myself!"

Again, Dad glanced at Mom, and she stared down at Cassie's head. And I figured if there was going to be any yelling, any angry blaming of the other one for what happened, it would have happened right then.

But it didn't. There was no yelling.

And something happy started blooming in me like a Roman candle flashing against the sky.

•Twenty-two•

"Pssssst!"

I was lying on the porch roof the next morning,
deep asleep. I'd been up till nearly dawn with Aunt
Caroline and Mom and Dad, having our family conference. When we'd finally turned in, Mom and Dad
had actually hugged each other. And then they'd
gone in together and stared for a long time at my
sisters.

"Psssssst!"

Sparky was making happy, jumpy sounds in the
yard just below me.

"What?" I half sat up, then fell back down, too
sleepy.

"Psssssst! Say, wake up now, boy! Hurry!"

I opened one eye a crack, then immediately
opened both eyes wide. Because inches from my
face, staring at me from a branch of the big elm tree,
was ugly old cross-eyed Pumpernickel. His bulk
nearly weighed the branch down to the roof.

"Get a move on, boy! Time's wasting!"

Had the cat said that? Nah, couldn't be. I was sleepy, but not sleepy enough to think a cat could speak English.

I scrambled to the edge of the roof, and below me, in the front yard, was Mrs. Beeson. Sparky was jumping eagerly around her knees.

"Come on!" she called up to me. "Your friend needs us!"

"Mike?" I asked, rubbing the hair out of my eyes and trying to get my bearings.

She shook her head, and it was then I saw she had worry sitting all over her, like an extra layer of skin.

"The other," she said quietly, mournfully.

Easy? My heart began thudding, and I kicked my sleeping bag in through the window, jerked on my shoes, and scrambled down the trellis. Pumpernickel raced me, sliding headfirst down the tree.

"What?" I asked when I hit the ground. "What's wrong with Ease?"

"I'll explain on the way to pick up Mike," she said. "Let's get moving."

As I shoved the tail of my T-shirt into my pants and fingercombed my hair, I realized the air was hazy with smoke, though the sky wasn't orange any longer. We walked along quickly—two people and two animals. A silent troupe, except for my questions.

"Did Easy go help with the fire?" I asked Mrs. Beeson in a rush. "Was it bad? What happened? Is your house completely gone?"

Curiosity was eating me alive, but she wouldn't be rushed.

Finally, after about a block, she stopped dead still and turned toward me. She planted both feet on the ground and leaned forward a little on her walking stick.

"This morning, very early, Easy Jack went to the fire," she said, staring into the distance. "He said he would be back directly, that he only wanted to find Judd. He said he figured Judd might have been out walking in the night, might need help getting home. But Easy Jack didn't come back to the Junglerama. Finally, I took my stick and went into town myself, to see what I could learn of what had happened to him."

She stopped cold, shaking her head. Finally, I reached out and touched her arm.

"Mrs. Beeson?"

"All the houses on my block were gone," she said, her voice full of creaking winds. "All burned, gone. And . . . and everyone working in the rubble looked stricken. Stricken with a deep, deep weariness and with a hurt. A heart hurt."

I swallowed hard and looked at Sparky.

"Judd died in the fire, boy. Folks said he had fallen asleep in the alley behind Thornberry Lane, and died of the smoke," Mrs. Beeson said then, so softly I had to strain to hear. "When the folks downtown gave him the sad news, I suppose your friend Easy Jack would have gone . . ."

". . . to the Emporium," I finished for her. The

day seemed suddenly unreal. Light seemed to be throbbing around the edges of things.

Judd, dead? It couldn't be. Not funny Judd, generous Judd.

"Easy's parents died when he was in kindergarten," I said, rambling, feeling numb. "He loved his uncle."

"Yes."

Neither of us talked the rest of the way to pick up Mike.

•　•　•

Mike and I knew exactly where Easy would be.

Whenever he wanted to be alone, so totally alone that even his tent wouldn't do, he always went to the quail shed. Once he told me that when he first moved to the Emporium, the year he was five, he went out there every afternoon and drew pictures of his mother.

When we reached the Emporium, Mrs. Beeson, Mike, Pumpernickel, Sparky, and I pushed open the gate of the chain-link fence and threaded our way through the pens and lean-tos till we came to the quail shed near the back corner of the property.

I could tell the second Mike pushed open the heavy wooden door and let a bright splotch of sunlight fall inside the dim building that Easy was there. I could tell by the way the quails were acting. They were quiet and worried, as though grieving along with him. Most of them had their heads tucked under their wings.

"Ease?" Mike called softly.

No answer.

Mike walked inside, and the rest of us followed and closed the door quietly.

"We won't bother you if you don't want, Ease," I said into the darkness. "We're just worried about you is all."

It was then we heard him sobbing, softly, muffled. The sound took our eyes to one corner of the room, and we saw him sitting on the dirt floor, slumped against the splintery wall.

We walked slowly in that direction. As we got close, Easy leaned forward, put his elbows on his knees and his head in his hands.

We all just stood staring at the ground, saying nothing, giving him space.

Suddenly, Easy jumped to his feet and began pacing furiously the small space between the wall and the nearest cage. He slammed one fist, hard, against a watering pan hanging on the wall.

"I'll never leave this place! Never!" Easy spat out, choking on the words. "I won't let Judd down like that. Judd loved these birds, and I'll never leave them, and nobody can make me! Never!"

Mike and I just stood there, useless. I felt miserable and couldn't figure out what to do.

"Those people downtown—they said I have to go live with some family," Easy went on, still pacing, still beside himself with grief and anger. "But nobody's going to take me out of here, off the Emporium! You understand me? Nobody! Judd would have relied on me to stay here and look after the birds, and nobody on earth can make me go! I'll spend the rest of my life here, protecting the birds like I couldn't protect my parents, or . . . Judd."

Then he went to the corner and put his hands on the two walls and stood there, his back to us, his shoulders heaving.

"Nobody can make me go," he whispered again, his voice cracking on the words.

I looked at Mike and he looked miserably back at me.

And then Mrs. Beeson stepped from the shadows behind us, where she had been standing. She walked over to within a couple of feet of Easy's back. The quails, who had gotten pretty shaken up since Easy began pacing, looked over to her and began cooing softly, as though they found some kind of reassurance in her presence, small and bent though she was.

"I don't suspect you know this, but Judd and I were good friends," she said softly to Easy.

He lifted his head, listening, probably surprised. I sure was, and Mike looked like he was, too.

"Midnight ramblers both, we were. And here of late we'd had some good visits, walking through this town together when others were abed."

Easy took his hands from the walls and turned around slowly, stood facing her with bruised-looking eyes.

"Oh, yes!" She laughed. "I had the utmost respect for your uncle, young Jack! He was a lover of nature, like myself. A gentle soul who watched a lot of life and had learned a thing or three from all that watching."

She took a step over and opened the biggest quail cage. A small brown bird jumped on her hand, and she took him gently from the cage. Outside its bars, the little bird jumped quickly onto her shoulder.

"Judd . . . Judd was the only one I ever saw who could get them to do that . . . ," Easy breathed, his pain-filled eyes glued on the bird. "For most people, they get scared and fly away."

Again, Mrs. Beeson laughed her ripples-running-over-rocks gravelly laugh.

"A wild thing knows who's out to capture and enslave it, and who, on the other hand, will be its friend. Judd was a kindred spirit to all things wild and free. And young Jack, he loved you. Oh, he talked of you with such pride, he did! You were where he centered his heart's dreams. He knew that you could do anything—anything!"

Jack's eyes flashed sparks again then, and he kicked hard at the wall and shook his head, his hands hard fists at his sides.

"I'll get those men who started that fire! I'll make them pay!" He was shaking all over. He moved to the window of the shed, and sobbed up toward the cloudy sky. "Do you hear me, Judd? I'll get them and make them pay!"

"No."

The way Mrs. Beeson said the single word made it feel like it slid sharply into each of us and stayed swirling around inside us. I don't think any of us dared to breathe. Mike and I turned like puppets toward her, listening. And Easy whirled back around from the window to look at her.

"Sheriff Perlman has arrested the men who threw the rock and knocked over my oil lamp and started the fire," she said quietly. "Now, young Jack, you must leave justice to the law because you have something far harder to do. You must find the way to live up to all that faith Judd had in you. And that way won't be found within these cages and fences. It's waiting somewhere outside, in the big world."

Easy just stared at Mrs. Beeson, frowning a little, concentrating I could tell. And she stepped a little closer to him, looked right up into his eyes.

"Jack, it's time you were brave enough to face the whole truth of this, to see the big picture. You've got to admit to yourself that Judd was partly the cause of his own death. He was a good man, a fine man. But he let superstitions grab onto him in his youth, and they haunted him all his life. They caused him to drink, and the drink was what really killed him. You know that, young Jack, now don't you?"

Easy didn't answer, but something changed a little in his face. Something shifted from anger to sadness, like the sunlight shifts to shadows. More tears started in his eyes, and he wiped them away with his arm. Not harshly now, not violently. Just slowly, with a shudder of grief in his shoulders.

Mrs. Beeson patted his arm, then stepped over to

the window. Gently, she took the quail from her shoulder in both hands, and held him up above her head.

The sun was playing hopscotch with the clouds—patterns of shadow fell across her face as we watched her offer the tiny bird through the open window to the sky.

"Fly free into this old world of pain and beauty," she whispered to the tiny quail. "Be strong now, and fly happily and free."

Then she opened her hands, and the little quail beat eager wings across the air toward the sun.

It made me smile to watch it.

And when I looked over at Easy he still had tears in his eyes, but he was smiling a little, too.

•Epilogue•

"Dog days" set in the second week of July. Sparky hates that term, but it's the only good way to describe the hot, muggy streak that always comes in the middle of Missouri summers. People move at half speed, even kids on bikes. And dogs like Sparky spend most of their time sleeping in the shade of some tree, their sides heaving as they dream of chasing rabbits in some cooler time and place.

This summer, the bulk of July was spent sort of wrestling things around and getting them back together from that strange Fourth of July weekend.

Mike's dad got the job managing the hardware store in Wasserville, and Mike's family sure enough got a crack at buying back their old house, without the land. They moved into it right about the middle of the month, and Easy Jack moved in with them. It's the perfect arrangement, when you think about it. Officially, Mike's parents are called Easy's foster parents now, but right from the day of Judd's funeral they've talked about wanting to adopt him.

It'll probably happen. All the kids think Mike and Easy have always acted about like brothers anyhow. Even Molly likes Easy, probably better than she likes Mike. Mike and Easy have Mike's huge old room to themselves, and they're fixing the attic up to be a science lab, or maybe a mini-basketball court. They haven't decided which for sure yet.

Mrs. Beeson moved into the Emporium, and is acting as caretaker for the birds. Mike and Easy give her a hand with the heavy work. The birds love her, anybody can see that. And her cats and the turkeys seem to get along fine, for some reason.

Mrs. Beeson even solved the problem of all the turkey mess that wouldn't come completely off the floor. She painted a huge sun (that looks exactly like a smiling grapefruit) all over it, disguising it completely.

• • •

And my family—well, we're moving to Kansas City.

We started driving up there three times a week right after my dad moved back. We're going to a family counselor Aunt Caroline arranged for us to see at one of the big hospitals there. It was after one of our sessions, when we stopped for ice cream on the way home, that my father found his new job. It was listed in a little free shopping magazine there in the ice cream place.

"Factory workers needed. Must have some meat-packing experience," he read out loud to my mother. She dropped her spoon into her butterscotch, snatched the magazine from him, and held it close to her face. She searched every word for the catch.

But there wasn't a catch. My dad drove back to the city the next day to apply for the job, and got it. Nobody here in Cloverton can believe the salary he'll be getting.

I guess lots of things in the city are going to be hard for us to believe for a while.

I don't know. I could be wrong about this, but I don't think Easy and Mike and Mrs. Beeson and I are the only ones that have had big changes happen in our lives since the Fourth. I kind of think the whole town has changed in a couple of ways.

I think, to begin with, the loss and return of Cassie and Judd's death and the fire made everybody feel a little ashamed. Ashamed of the way we'd got panicky and allowed words of anger and hatred to take some root in our town.

I think even Carl and Daryl Tyler felt some of that shame.

We were feeding the animals at the Junglerama one day a couple of weeks ago when they showed up, carrying a half-grown garter snake in a bucket. Daryl handed it to Easy, as a gift.

"We don't see much of Matt no more," he said, looking at the ground. "He was getting . . . you know. Weird."

"We're sorry about that," Daryl added, clearing his throat. "About that business with those snakes of yours. We shouldn't have ought to let him talk us into helping with it."

Easy shrugged and smiled, accepting the bucket and the apology. And I think we all three knew that was the end of our worries with Matt's gang. Abandoned, Matt wouldn't be a threat. Bullies need their backers.

Besides feeling a little ashamed, though, I think everybody in Cloverton felt, on the other hand, a little proud. Proud of the way everybody banded together to search for Cass, and of how they'd organized to fight the fire. No matter how tough things get in the town of Cloverton, I think it'll be a while before people forget again how much they care about each other.

· · ·

So today I'm packing up my closet, and it feels like summer's ending early even though August only started a week ago. Tomorrow we'll take the first load of stuff to our new house in Kansas City, and by the end of the week we'll be about completely moved.

Later today Mike and Easy and I are getting together, so I've got to remember to take this Traveling Fund money so we can divvy it up. There's no reason for a traveling fund anymore.

Because yesterday, we released the animals from the Junglerama.

They were getting bored. They'd been caged long enough. There was even some danger that the heat might affect them, especially the lizards. They were getting pretty dry-looking, in spite of all the pans of water we kept giving them.

It was sort of a mutual decision to release them, made on the spur of the moment.

Yesterday morning we were cleaning out the supply barrel outside the trailer, and Mike came up with handfuls of ladies' fingers and a Roman candle. It was the firecrackers we'd bought and then not used in all the excitement of the Fourth.

"Well, look here what we forgot," he said. "Do we save them for next year?"

Easy and I just stood looking at them.

"Or do we use them for something else?" Mike finished.

"It's time, isn't it?" Easy said, his voice husky. "Time to let the animals go."

And Mike and I nodded, knowing that it was.

So each of us took something—a cage of turtles or a tub of baby frogs or an armload of fireworks or the cage of skinks or the new garter snake—and we carried them all in just two trips across the soybean field, back to the woods.

By the time the cages were lined up on the bank of the stream, the shadows were long through the oak trees. It was a sad time of day. All of us felt it, I know.

"You'll be back to visit a lot, Teej," Mike said.

"Sure," I answered, clearing my throat. "And you guys won't believe this. There's a pitching camp right about a few blocks from our new house."

I was pretty sure I'd already told them that, at least a few times, but I said it again for something to say anyway. And Mike and Easy acted impressed, again.

And then there wasn't anything else to do. The Roman candle was set up and aimed over the trees, across the water.

It was time.

Nobody looked at anybody else.

"Mrs. Beeson told me that Judd was a kindred spirit to the wild things of the world," Easy said. "That's us, too, okay? We're kindred spirits of the wild things, and of each other, no matter where we are, right?"

"Right!" Mike and I shouted.

A small wind came up, barely moving the thick, glossy oak leaves.

"It was a neat place," Mike said.

"The best," I quickly agreed.

"I always felt like things were great when we were out here with the animals," Mike continued slowly. "I mean, they didn't ask much, and they were always so alive, you know? Like when everything else was so confusing, in the Junglerama things were just so neat."

"So powerful," I added. "So strong."

Nobody said anything else then. After a couple of minutes, Easy crouched beside the lizard cage.

"Okay . . . ," he whispered. Then he reached out with his long fingers and grabbed the latch. "Now!"

And Mike and I followed, quickly releasing all the reptiles out into the summer world.

They scattered, they scampered. They didn't look back, except for Rex. He turned and looked at us with his chin tilted sideways, then he scampered, too.

I kept my eyes on one of the turtles, as it swam chunkily into the stream, the red on its neck like a flash of energy jolting through the clear water.

And then I knelt and lit the Roman candle. Its balls of colored fire soared over the stream and punched into the sky, filling everything around us with energy and color and life.

And it was then I saw it—the big picture. I saw it, and I knew from the looks on their faces that Easy and Mike saw it, too. And I figured it would probably stay inside our heads forever, no matter what.

For those few seconds, all the world looked wild and colorful and wonderful and free. Not safe, not perfect, not easy. No, but wonderful, throbbing, and glowing. I could see it was just waiting, rolling itself out in all directions from us, filled with power and possibilities.

All the world in every direction became a junglerama.